Set Loose
Isabel Morin

Chapter One

Emily Chase sat in a cramped waiting room somewhere off the highway in Las Vegas, listlessly paging through a year-old issue of *Newsweek*. She looked up when the grizzled old mechanic came in, wiping his brow like a surgeon with bad news for the waiting family.

"Your transmission's gone," he said without preamble.

"That's more or less the worst news I could get, right?" she asked.

"Afraid so."

"But it can be fixed? It's not dead?"

"Sure, we can fix it, but I'll need to order parts. It's too late to get anything done today and then we got the weekend and Labor Day. We're looking at next Thursday or Friday, and it'll run you about two thousand dollars."

Jesus. She'd been braced for something bad, but not that bad. She was already broke, so this would have to go on her last non-maxed out credit card, a thought that caused an instant stomachache. When was her downward slide going to end?

Even before her injury she wouldn't have been able to afford this. Ballet looked glamorous from the seats but the pay was barely adequate, even for soloists like she'd been, and living in San Francisco wasn't cheap. And she wasn't even a dancer anymore, just an injured ex-dancer with no job, no prospects, and collection agencies calling her on a regular basis.

"Okay. Go ahead and fix it," she said, wondering if she was making an enormous mistake.

"Want me to call you a cab?" he asked, and she nodded her head and thanked him, then went out to her car where she rummaged through her belongings, moving items into the two bags she'd take with her. She'd have to leave everything else there – pretty much everything she owned in the world– and hope no one took anything.

Maybe she should junk the car and fly to Boston, but she wasn't ready to face her friends and family when she was still such a mess. A plane ride was too quick. She needed the process of driving and all those hours to ruminate. Besides, she'd still need a car when she got there. Either way she'd be spending money she didn't have.

The cab arrived and she stared out the window as they drove, taking in the enormous restaurants, clubs and hotels on Las Vegas Boulevard. She'd never been here before, but she could tell the driver was taking her to the touristy part of the city. It didn't look like what she'd imagined though because it was still full daylight, too hot for people to be out walking around. The sidewalks were almost deserted and the buildings looked tired instead of glitzy.

The taxi pulled to a stop in front of the Luxor hotel.

"I'm pretty sure I won't be able to afford any of the hotels around here," Emily said, leaning forward to talk to the driver. She had asked him to drop her off someplace decent and affordable. The giant pyramid rising into the sky wasn't what she had in mind.

"Sure you can," he said, turning around to look at her. "These places are as cheap as a motel you'd find anywhere else. Especially the ones that have their own casinos, like this one. They figure it's better for you to have money in your pocket to gamble. Trust me, I know what I'm talking about."

Too tired to argue, she paid him and grabbed her bags. The heat hit her full force as she got out of the air-conditioned cab, her tank top and skirt sticking to her as she made for the entrance. She was miserable and expecting more disappointment, but the driver was right. Though the weekend rates were too steep for her, averaged together with the cheap weekday rates it would only cost her sixty dollars a night.

Her room was on the twenty-second floor, and when she stepped inside her jaw dropped. It was enormous, with a king-sized bed and sitting area done in royal blue and cream, and a huge bathroom with a sunken Jacuzzi tub. Maybe her week wouldn't be so terrible after all. Exhausted, she fell back on the bed and turned on the TV.

She didn't leave the hotel all weekend. It was over a hundred degrees outside, she had about a thousand channels for her viewing pleasure, and the hotel was like its own small city, complete with five different restaurants, a food court, plus a bunch of bars and nightclubs.

Not that she did much besides watch TV. Where most people would have been running around town, Emily lay in bed for hours, remote control in hand, catching up on all the shows and movies she'd never had the time to see.

Sunday night she was lying in bed in a t-shirt and underwear when her cell phone rang. Probably her mom calling to check in.

"Hello," she said, her eyes still glued to "Say Yes to the Dress." What was with these women, anyway?

"Emily?" It sounded like someone she ought to know, a friendly female voice, but she couldn't quite place it.

"Yes?"

The voice was suddenly all business. "I'm calling on behalf of Bank of America. As I believe you're aware, you are now ninety days delinquent in your payments to us. If you do not –"

Emily hung up the phone and sat there, breathing hard. The collection agency had always called her landline before. How had they gotten this number?

She couldn't seem to catch her breath. Lightheaded, she sat on the edge of the bed and folded over, letting her head hang between her knees. When she sat up again she stared at the phone like a snake had suddenly crawled into her bed.

What the hell she was going to do?

After the ballet company let her go she'd had to live off her credit cards. But she'd stayed in San Francisco, desperately certain that her foot would recover and she'd prove everyone wrong. It had been foolish and delusional, and now she was paying for it.

If only she could go back and replay that one jump, that one bad landing, everything would be different. She'd be living the life she was supposed to have instead of this nightmare.

Once again she replayed it in her head – the sheer joy of soaring through the air ending with the unmistakable pop of her Achilles tendon rupturing, the sudden pain that dropped her to the floor.

Those few seconds of her life played over and over on a never-ending loop, one she couldn't change no many how many times it ran.

She needed to get out.

Getting up she pulled the first thing she saw out of her bag. Then she stood and stared at the red strapless dress she used to wear to opening night galas. Fine, she'd wear this. She might as well look her best even if her life was crumbling around her.

Standing in front of the full-length mirror in her dress and heels, she pulled her long blond hair into a ponytail and dragged red lipstick across her mouth. She didn't look half bad. If no one looked her in the eye, they'd never know how desperate she was.

Once out on the sidewalk she stood there, looking around. The city definitely looked a lot better at night all lit up, and the heat was tolerable. She breathed deeply, turned left and started walking.

The Strip was a bit of a let down, just hotels and casinos, each one over-the-top in its own way. But she had no money to spare and wouldn't know how to gamble even if she did, so the casinos were out. That left eating, but she'd already had a cheap taco dinner from the hotel food court.

She stood uncertainly on the sidewalk a block or so from her hotel. Now that she was outside, the unfamiliar city felt unnerving, yet another unknowable thing in her life. Maybe instead of working so hard to feel better she should go back to her room, turn off the phone and numb her brain with more television.

Paralyzed by indecision, a trait she'd only recently developed, she stood rooted to the sidewalk for several minutes. Only gradually did she become aware of the stream of people heading into a nearby doorway. Looking up, she realized she was standing in front of the Pink Pussycat Gentleman's Club. A neon sign complete with sexy pink cat lured people in.

She'd never been in a strip club before. The idea of them had always both repelled and intrigued her. This one didn't look seedy though. It was right on the main drag and the people going in were well-dressed.

What the hell? She'd always been curious. Besides, she wanted to get out of her head. What better place to be distracted than here?

The twenty-dollar cover charge was steeper than she expected, but she paid it anyway, determined now. Moving along with the crowd, she looked around, trying to take it all in – the loud music, people yelling and catcalling. A smiling hostess in a black, body-hugging dress came up to her and asked if she wanted a table.

"Would it be all right if I just stand around and watch?"

"Sure, honey. You're here alone?"

Emily nodded, hoping she didn't look as lost as she felt. "Yes. This was kind of an impulsive visit."

"Nothing wrong with that. We're all about impulses here. I hope you see something you like," she said, giving a wink before turning to a group of businessmen who'd just arrived.

Emily let out a sigh of relief at having passed the first trial. Now she needed a drink. Spotting the bar on the other side of the room, she slowly made her way through the crowd, all the while trying to convince herself she had no reason to feel uncomfortable. Which wasn't easy considering the attention she was getting. There were more women than she would have expected if she'd given this any thought at all, but that wasn't saying much. The audience was still overwhelmingly male, and they had no problem making their interest known with looks, smiles and requests to stop and talk. Emily smiled and kept moving.

Even after she made it to the bar it took a while to get her drink. The bartenders were all scantily clad women who seemed more inclined to wait on the men, but eventually she got her gin and tonic. Scoping the room out, she decided to watch from the edge of the crowd, where she could see the action without being a part of it.

Several women, naked but for their thongs, were circulating among the tables and standing customers while another dancer was on stage stripping to the AC/DC song "You Shook Me," her garters thick with bills. The stage extended out into the audience and had a pole at the end of it. Men filled the seats running along the edge, every one of them clutching money as they stared with rapt attention.

Emily watched just as raptly as the dancer moved to the pole where she swung around it with the precision of a gymnast. She had decent presence, worked the whole stage well and looked like she was having a good time.

I could do that.

The thought popped into Emily's head, and once it did she couldn't help but imagine herself up there. Which was crazy. No way could she really do that.

Could she?

Just as she was contemplating the idea, a stripper stopped at a table about ten feet in front of her, climbed onto a guy's lap and started grinding on him. Emily stood there, feeling like a pervert for watching but unable to look away. It just seemed so...private. But even as her face heated in mortification, her body was humming with awareness. Her nipples were tight buds, her underwear damp, and her breath was coming fast and light.

The woman ground faster and faster, her long dark hair whipping around as the man stared at her with rapt attention. Then she slid off him and stood by while he slid a fifty-dollar bill into her thong.

Forget how turned on she was. Her head spun at the amount of money these women must make in one night. Even if she never did a lap dance, and she wasn't sure she could, a few weeks of this sort of cash and her most pressing problem would be solved.

Maybe this wasn't what she'd trained all those years for, but it was still dancing. She'd danced in front of audiences all around the world, audiences that expected perfection from every role she performed. She could dance anything. Surely she could play the part of a sexy stripper? All she had to do was stick around Vegas a little longer than she'd planned. She'd had to scrape to come up with September's rent for a room in an apartment in Boston, so it would be a shame not to be living in it, but at least she knew it would be waiting for her when she got there. Besides, this way she'd have money for October's rent as well.

As crazy as it sounded even in her head, the chance to make enough money to get out of debt and back on her feet was too good to pass up. Besides, she wasn't self-conscious about her body the way most women were. She'd spent too long thinking of it as her instrument, dressing around other dancers, both men and women, for years. Male partners and ballet masters and choreographers had been putting their hands on her all her life and it had never fazed her a bit.

Determined now, she headed back toward the entrance, figuring the hostess could advise her how to get an audition. She was so focused that at first she didn't hear the drunk guy talking to her. By the time did hear him, he was standing right in front of her, blocking her way.

"Hey, sweetheart. You're not leaving yet, are you?" he asked, his beer breath blowing in her face.

"I need to talk to someone."

"You are talking to someone. Me," he said, and then laughed like he'd said something incredibly clever.

"Excuse me, I really need to go."

"I saw you watching the girls. Is that what you like?" he asked, as if she hadn't spoken.

"I'd like to be left alone, actually," Emily said, her temper flaring.

She needed to get away from this creep. Unfortunately, a group of guys started to push their way through just as she was trying to escape and she didn't get anywhere.

"Come on, lighten up," the creep said, reaching out and grabbing her arm.

Emily tried to pull away from him. "Look, I'm not interested."

"Take it easy. All I want to do is talk," he said, his grip tightening.

Now what was she supposed to do? Call for help? Hit him? This was crazy. Emily was looking around, wondering if she'd have to cause a scene, when a man pushed through the crowd and grabbed the creep's shoulder with an air of professional intimidation.

"That's it, buddy. You're out of here," he said.

"What? You can't do that. I'm here with a bunch of people."

"Then I guess you'd better say your goodbyes. You've got exactly thirty seconds. Starting now."

The creep shot the bouncer a malevolent look and hurried over to his friends, saying something while darting a glance backward. Then he was out the door. Emily let out the breath she'd been holding and turned to her rescuer, finally taking him in.

Oh my.

He was probably a couple of inches over six feet, like any respectable bouncer would be, but lean and hard rather than bulky. Native American, with nut-brown skin and straight black hair that slid across his high cheekbones and just brushed the nape of his neck. He was dressed like the other bouncers in dark pants and a white button-down shirt rolled to the elbows, and just the sight of his muscled forearms nearly sent her into a swoon.

His dark, thickly lashed eyes were focused on her.

"Thanks," she said, her voice breathier than usual. "He really wasn't taking no for an answer."

"No thanks necessary. I love throwing guys like that out." He looked at her curiously. "If you don't mind my saying, you seem out of place here. Like you were looking for the opera or something."

"What makes you say that?" Emily asked, irrationally annoyed. "I'm perfectly comfortable here. And I'm not the only woman who's dressed up."

"It's not what you're wearing, exactly," he said, looking uncomfortable now, probably wishing he hadn't said anything. "You carry yourself differently. Like maybe you ran away from the castle to see how the rabble live."

Emily stared at him, not knowing what to say. God knew she was no princess. She was broke and jobless and didn't even have a college degree since she went straight from high school into the Boston corps de ballet. But it just showed what good posture could do for a person. Or maybe all those years playing princesses on stage had rubbed off.

"I'm afraid not," she finally said. "I'm just well-dressed rabble."

This triggered a smile from him that sent unexpected heat into her cheeks and belly. Standing this close to him, she could tell how powerful his body was, his strength brought under control by what appeared to be a steely disposition. Was she imagining the flicker of interest in his eyes as he took her in so thoroughly?

The mood broke when he looked at something over her head. "Damn. I have to go." He looked back down at her, his expression serious and thoughtful. "You have a good night. Give a shout if you get into any trouble," he said, squeezing her arm before heading off.

Emily watched him make his way through the crowd and between tables to a customer who'd gotten too friendly during a lap dance. He leaned over and said a few words and the man's hands fell away from the stripper's breasts. Then he continued on, moving around the room, his gaze taking everything in.

Clearly he had his hands full rescuing damsels in distress.

Only when he'd disappeared from view did Emily remember what she'd been doing before getting waylaid. The hostess was nowhere to be seen, but one of the dancers passed by, a pretty redhead who was probably even prettier without all the make-up.

"Excuse me," Emily said, but the music was so loud the woman didn't so much as turn her head.

Emily moved after her, touching her lightly on the shoulder. Her skin was oiled and sprinkled with glitter, her eyes wary when she turned.

Emily let her hand drop and tried her best not to look at the woman's naked breasts. "Excuse me. Could I ask you a question?"

"That depends."

"I was wondering if you could tell me how I'd go about getting an audition."

The dancer's eyes widened in surprise and then she smiled. "See that stocky guy standing by the VIP door? That's Steve, the manager. Talk to him and he'll tell you if he's interested."

Emily followed her gaze to a barrel-chested guy, probably Italian, standing across the room. "Thanks, I appreciate it," she said. Then, because she was beginning to realize that time was money, she pulled out her wallet and handed the woman a ten-dollar bill. She smiled in thanks, tucked the money into her thong, and headed back into the sea of men.

Taking a deep breath and ignoring the flutter of nerves in her belly, Emily made her way over to the manager.

"Hi there," she said, then inwardly winced. God, she sounded like she was trying to pick him up.

Steve-the-manager looked at her with a generic smile. "What can I do for you, sweetheart?"

Her heart beat like mad now and her palms were damp. "I'd like to audition."

"Is that so?" he said, taking the statement as invitation to look her up and down. She'd been checked out more tonight than she had in the last ten years put together. "Sorry, babe. Nothing personal, but your tits are too small and men like their strippers naughty. You're pretty but you're not the right type."

"I can dance better than anyone in here, and I can act naughty."

"Is that so?" Steve asked, crossing his arms over his chest with a doubtful smirk.

He wasn't buying it. Her throat tightened as the panic she'd been suppressing threatened to rear its ugly head again. She had to prove she had what it took before he lost interest in her entirely.

She had to show him.

She swung her left leg out and up in a wide arc until her ankle rested on his shoulder and the silky skirt of her dress slid down her thigh. Grabbing him by the bicep, she pressed against him until her pelvis was up against his. Then slowly, one hand gripping his belt while the other rested on her breasts, she arched backwards, lower and lower until she was upside down, her hair streaming towards the floor. Her breasts practically popped out of her dress but she hung there another few seconds before slowly rising back up to meet his gaze with a saucy smile.

One of his hands was resting on her hip, his other arm cradled her thigh. His erection pressed against her, which skeeved her out but also proved that she'd made her point. Swinging her leg back down to the floor she stepped back and straightened her skirt.

"So how about that audition?"

The manager blinked once and then regained his composure, though he looked slightly pissed.

"Come back tomorrow at six. If you bomb I don't want it to be during prime time."

"I never bomb," Emily replied, turning away before he could see her triumphant grin.

She faltered for a moment when she caught sight of the hot bouncer standing a few yards away, watching her with a look she couldn't read. Whatever it was, he'd obviously caught her impromptu tryout. Too bad she hadn't been able to try out on him. Now *that* would have been something.

Unsure what to do, she gave him a smile and a little wave. If he hadn't believed she was rabble before, her little show should have done the trick.

***

Cutter stood across the room, unable to believe his eyes. The gorgeous blond was grinding against Steve, her long, lithe body moving like a pro. Better than most pros, as a matter of fact. Was she a professional stripper? If so, his reading of her had been all wrong. She'd seemed way too unsure of herself to have worked in a strip club before.

Jesus, her legs. He watched as her dress slid down and her sleek, muscled thighs parted, pressing against Steve as she went into a backbend. In the blink of an eye she'd gone from a delicately pretty woman to a fantasy, her eyes closed and face set as if she were in ecstasy.

What he wouldn't give to be Steve right now.

He watched, unable to take his eyes off her as she pulled herself back up and stood in front of the manager. Then she stepped back and was all business, her hand on her hip as if she hadn't just been climbing all over the guy. But then, Cutter was used to watching women pretend they were in the throes of desire. Knowing they were faking it was the reason he was able to do his job without a constant hard-on. They might occasionally be having a good time, but it was work, and the hotter they made the audience, the more money they made.

But what was she doing acting that way with Steve?

She and the manager exchanged a few words and then she turned away, a pleased smile on her face. The smile faded when she saw Cutter and she hesitated, looking uncertain. For a second he thought she might come over, but no such luck. She gave a tentative smile and a little wave and strode away.

Cutter watched her go, her hips swaying beneath the red dress. He wasn't the only one who noticed her passing, either. In a room with naked women up on stage and strolling through the crowd, she still managed to catch the eye of every man she passed.

He headed across the floor to where the manager still stood. Steve glanced over at him and nodded, his eyes taking in everything that went on around him – the dancers, the audience, the crowd at the bar.

"So what was all that about?" Cutter asked, trying to sound casual.

"What was what about?"

"That woman climbing all over you a minute ago."

"You caught that, did you? Some girls won't take no for an answer."

"You mean she was hitting on you?" Cutter asked, disappointment shooting through him.

"You don't need to sound so damn surprised. Anyway, she wasn't hitting on me, she was auditioning. She'll be back tomorrow to dance. If she doesn't chicken out, that is."

"Dancing? Here?" A quick rush of pleasure ran through him at the thought of seeing her again, followed directly by dismay as his protective instincts kicked in. A woman like her shouldn't be stripping in front of a roomful of drunks.

"That's right. We'll see if she can make the whole goddamn room as hard as she made me. Jesus Christ."

Looking disgusted with himself, as if he ought to be able to control all such reactions by now, Steve walked away, grumbling under his breath.

Cutter stood where he was, barely breathing. Tomorrow night he'd get to see the rest of that incredible body, every inch of those endless, perfect legs. If he ever got a hold of her he was going to start at the bottom and lick his way up.

Then he caught himself. What the hell was he thinking? He didn't touch the dancers. He protected them from guys who looked at them the way he'd just been looking. Christ. This girl would need his help more than any of them. The men were going to love her, and he was going to have to work his ass off to keep everyone at bay.

So fine. Tomorrow night the classy blond was going to get naked on stage. It was going to be a goddamn beautiful sight, and he would try his damnedest not to care.

Chapter Two

"Gin and tonic please."

At five o'clock the next evening Emily's confidence had waned considerably and her stomach was churning like it used to before a performance, the difference being that tonight she was fortifying herself with some liquid courage from one of the hotel bars. As she nursed her drink she reviewed the choreography she'd worked out earlier in the day.

She was most nervous about the pole since she had no way to practice. She was pretty much going to wing that part. Maybe she'd slide up and down as if terribly excited by its phallic nature and hope she didn't look too ridiculous.

In the duffel bag at her feet were all the things she'd bought that afternoon – thong, garters, four-inch black heels, gold glitter, the works. In the shower she'd become acutely aware of every hair on her body and how it would be seen close-up and personal if she didn't remove it, which led to a painful appointment with a Brazilian wax. If she didn't at least make back what she'd spent today she was going to be seriously bummed.

She stuck to one gin and tonic since she was such a lightweight and was worried that the combination of liquor, nerves and dancing would end in her vomiting in the middle of her routine. Or what if she fell off the pole or was generally so unsexy that she was booed or laughed at?

Almost as nerve-wracking as the situation itself was the thought of the bouncer seeing her up there. Which was ridiculous since there'd be a whole roomful of strangers she needed to impress, and she knew him only slightly better than she knew them.

But it had been a long time since she'd felt any interest in a man. She'd been too focused on her career, and more recently too confused, to get involved with anyone.

The club was a lot quieter when she arrived than it had been last night. A dancer was on stage but the audience was small and its response lackluster. There was no way to know which came first, the lack of interest or the low energy dance, but Emily sincerely hoped she got a little more love or it was going to be hard to maintain a brave face.

The bouncer was there and her heart gave a little leap at the sight of him. He came over to where she was standing, his expression serious.

"I hear you're auditioning. You sure you want to do that?"

"Why wouldn't I?" she asked, taken aback.

"No need to get defensive. It's a tough job, that's all, and it can do a number on you. I've seen it happen and it's not pretty."

Emily wasn't sure how to respond. No doubt he was right, but she wasn't a fragile flower. And anyway, she wouldn't be around long enough to worry about that sort of thing.

"I appreciate your concern, but you don't need to worry about me. I'm a lot tougher than I look."

'Is that right?" he asked, looking skeptical.

"Yes, that is right," Emily said, enunciating clearly because the gin and tonic had hit her full on and she was suddenly aware of every syllable as it tried to make its way out of her mouth. Clearly she wasn't tough enough to handle tonight without a little outside help, but he didn't have to know that. "I really ought to get ready," she continued. "If you would just point me toward the dressing room..."

She started to teeter, and she wasn't even wearing her stilettos yet. Maybe she should have gone a bit easier on the booze, or at least eaten something.

"Easy there, tiger," he said, the mischievous smile tugging at his mouth changing his entire expression. His eyes glinted with humor and he was suddenly so sexy Emily lost her balance again. His big, warm hand on her arm steadied her but sent her nervous system into overdrive.

"What's your name?" he asked.

"Me?"

"Yes, you." His smile was wider now, the gleam in his eye more intense.

"Emily. Emily Chase. And yours?" she asked, striving for dignity. She drew herself up even straighter to demonstrate her regal posture.

"Cutter Lawrence, at your service. Head to the back of the room there, under that exit sign, and you'll see the dressing rooms."

"Wonderful, thank you."

"Think nothing of it," he said, and she could have sworn he was trying not to laugh.

Turning away from him, Emily hurried toward the door he pointed out, trying to focus, to get into her role the way she always did before a show. Clearly she should be channeling her attraction to Cutter into her performance.

The dressing room was comfy and innocuous. She wasn't exactly sure what she'd been expecting, but there was nothing shocking on display. Just a sagging blue sofa set against one wall, a couple of armchairs and folding chairs, and a big mirror on one white wall with a counter running beneath it. Another wall held rows of lockers, and there was a doorway that led to a bathroom and shower. Only the rack of costumes and the dangerously high-heeled shoes scattered here and there gave away the fact that strippers were in residence.

The space was empty but for one woman, the redhead she'd spoken to the night before. She was in full costume – catholic schoolgirl, a true classic – but without the makeup, and she looked younger than she had last night. Twenty-two, maybe twenty-three.

Emily stopped nervously in the doorway, bracing herself with one hand, and the redhead glanced up, her surprised look turning to one of recognition.

"Hey, there. Come on in," she said, sitting up and smiling. "I wondered if you'd be back."

Emily stepped into the room, still gripping her bag. "I wondered that myself," she said, trying to smile. "I'm pretty nervous, or I was before I got myself drunk."

"Well, you've already taken care of step number one. Clearly you have good instincts. Anyway, you don't need to be scared. Men are easy. Why don't you get dressed and then I'll give you a few pointers. My name's Cheryl, by the way."

Emily smiled gratefully and introduced herself, then set about smoothing shimmery lotion over every inch of skin. Next she put on her sexy librarian costume – white blouse, tweed skirt, even a pair of fake horn-rimmed glasses. Underneath all that she wore red lace underwear. It was a bit garish for her own taste, but then her own taste would bore everyone to tears.

When she was fully dressed she studied her reflection – not exactly the Swan Queen, but she'd do. Sitting on a stool in front of the mirror she took out her cosmetics bag and began to make up her face. Luckily she'd been doing her own stage makeup for years and was pretty good at it. Even freaked out and drunk she managed to make her eyes sultry and dark-lashed, her mouth fuller than it really was and deep red.

Some of the girls wore wigs, but since her hair was long and thick and wigs were hot and itchy, she'd decided to go with her own hair. She teased it around the crown until it was full and reminiscent of a Victoria's Secret model, then smoothed it until it was sleek and slid over her shoulders when she shook her head.

She was planning to throw her hair around a lot tonight, but not until she took it out of her librarian's bun, so she twisted it into a loose knot and secured it with a pencil. Then she pulled on her garters and looked at herself in the mirror.

A feeling of unreality washed over her as she looked at the stranger reflected back at her. Who was she really, when her entire identity had been based on her life as a ballerina? Would a few weeks here make her nothing more than a hard-up stripper? Would she even recognize herself anymore?

"You look great. How do you feel?" Cheryl said, coming over to inspect her.

"Pretty bizarre, actually."

"Try not to think too much. This will help," Cheryl said, pulling a flask out of her bag.

Emily wasn't sure drinking even more would cure what ailed her, but she was willing to try. A few sips later her she was able to look at herself without having an existential panic attack.

She'd stretched and warmed-up in her hotel room, but that was a while ago now. Kicking off her heels she pulled on a pair of pink legwarmers, grabbed a folding chair for her makeshift barre, and began to move – plié, grand plié, the familiar motions soothing her until she was in her zone.

Two other women wearing only thongs and money came in, their laughter fading as they looked at her in surprise. Emily recognized the tall one as the dancer who'd been on when she came in.

"This is Emily. She's trying out tonight," Cheryl explained.

"You sure you're in the right place?" the tall one asked, her voice sharp. She was pretty in an angular way but her eyes were hard, like maybe she'd been around the block a few times. "This ain't the ballet."

Emily had been a bit nervous about how she'd get along with the other women, but she wasn't about to let anyone push her around. She'd been dealing with whole companies of competitive dancers since she was a teenager and knew how to hold her own.

"Yes, I'm sure," she said, looking the woman in the eye. "This is my first time and I'm trying not to freak out. This relaxes me."

Admitting she was scared did the trick. The woman smiled and came the rest of the way into the room. "I'm Nancy," she said, kicking her heels off and taking a sip from Cheryl's flask. "This is Tina," she said, gesturing to her friend, a petite Hispanic woman who glanced up to say hi before typing something on her phone.

Emily let the women's chatter float around her. By the time she was done with her warm-up she felt relatively calm and centered, as if she'd just meditated. Pulling her heels back on, she sat down on one of the chairs to wait.

"So what brings you to our little slice of paradise?" Nancy asked.

"I *was* a professional ballet dancer until I landed wrong and hurt my foot. Now I'm broke and need to figure out what to do with the rest of my life."

"Wow, it's like *Flashdance*, only in reverse."

Emily groaned and let her head fall into her hands. "Oh God, you're right. All I need is my welder's license. Maybe that's what I should do next."

"Nah. I'd skip all that and go straight for the rich older guy."

Nancy and Tina headed back out to work the floor and other women started to filter in, some coming on shift, others on their way out. Emily introduced herself to them if they looked curious, but mostly she listened as Cheryl filled her in on everything she needed to know. Like the fact that they each danced for three songs and you needed to have your breasts on display by the end of the first song and be down to your thong by the end of the second. Then you just showed it all off and raked in the money during the last song. Luckily, she had pretty much figured all that out last night and had planned her dances accordingly.

Her injury wouldn't pose a problem for the kind of dancing she'd be doing tonight, so there was that to be thankful for. Mostly she had to stay away from jumps and extended periods on her left leg. Ironically, she felt better now than she did when she was still with the company. Back then she had too many aches and pains to count. She'd also gained close to ten pounds since she no longer danced seven hours a day.

The extra weight was probably a good thing as far as stripping was concerned, since the gaunt look wasn't too sexy.

At six-thirty Cheryl went on and Emily followed to watch her from the wings. She also gave her song selection to Stan, the audio guy.

She'd chosen three of her favorite songs, the ones she liked to dance to alone in her apartment. She'd start out with Nina Simone's "I Want a Little Sugar in My Bowl," then "Son of a Preacher Man" by Dusty Springfield, and finally "Little Red Corvette." That way she'd start off slow and work up to a nice frenzy. Maybe they were a bit old school, but she wanted to dance to music that made her feel sexy. She'd always preferred soul and blues when she wasn't listening to classical.

"What's your stage name, sweetheart?" Stan asked. A skinny guy of indeterminate age who looked like he smoked about five packs a day, he was also in charge of announcing the dancers.

Emily hadn't even thought about a stage name.

"Um, Star?"

"Why not?" he shrugged. 'We don't have any others right now."

Okay, so it wasn't very original, but it sounded like a stripper name. It also had a nice layer of irony that only she understood.

Before she knew it, it was her turn to go on. Her legs were shaking and her heart slammed frantically in her chest, but even the attack of nerves felt good in a way, since she'd never expected to perform again. She knew how to do nerves. How many nights had she waited in the wings to go on, terrified she'd screw up?

So she counted out her entrance and then walked out onto the stage in time with the slow, sensual music, a woman arriving home from work, moving dreamily as she unbuttoned her demure white blouse. Stopping in the middle of the stage she let it slide off and fall to the floor, revealing her red lace bra. She ran her hands down her breasts and over her hips, as if she were thinking of someone else's hands.

Then she caught sight of Cutter. He stood in the middle of the room, those dark eyes following her around the stage. But instead of feeling self-conscious or embarrassed, the thought of turning him on sent an electric thrill through her.

She was no longer pretending. It was his hands she wanted on her, his mouth. Her movements became more sinuous, a private seduction played out in front of everyone.

The crowd was making noise, hooting and calling out, clapping for her. She pulled the pencil out of her hair and shook it so that it swirled around her shoulders. Swinging her hips she spun as she unclasped her bra, letting one strap and then the other slide over her shoulders before letting the whole thing fall.

She moved faster as a sense of freedom, of total abandon swept through her. She danced without worrying about perfect technique or what her line looked like. This was primitive, like dancing around the fire or praying for rain.

The second song was building toward the finish when she teased the zipper on her skirt down, driving everyone wild to see what was underneath. Standing at the very tip of the stage, Emily looked right at Cutter and let the skirt drop. Her smile was wicked, daring him to think she didn't have what it took. He watched her every move, his eyes following the skirt down her legs, then back up until his heated gaze held hers.

For the space of a few heartbeats she forgot to move, held by the grim desire she saw there, as if he'd look away if he could. Breaking eye contact, she kicked the skirt to the side just as "Little Red Corvette" started to play. A song made for stripping, it propelled her across the stage until she spun fast and wicked, her kicks higher, her hips moving with every beat.

Men crowded around the stage, leaning forward with money in their hands. Emily moved closer to them and several men at once tucked bills into her thong. Even though she'd been expecting it, she had to resist the urge to pull away from their strange hands and hungry, even desperate looks. Then the moment passed and she was Star again, prancing along the edge, kneeling down and slithering along. It was all part of the game, and she did her part, tossing them a wink and a naughty smile before moving to the other side of the stage.

She whirled around as the song built toward its climax, her movements faster and more urgent, mimicking the urgency before release. Without even planning it she grabbed hold of the pole and spun around it, surprised by how easy it was, another toy to tease the crowd, tease Cutter.

The song wound down and she worked the perimeter again, letting men cop a feel as they thrust everything from one to twenty dollar bills at her. Then it was over. Tossing her hair one last time, she left the stage.

Stan looked up from the audio equipment. "Not bad, kid."

"Thanks," she smiled, her body still humming. "Hopefully it was good enough for Steve."

"Oh, it will be. That was good enough for anyone."

Cheryl ran in from the floor to give her a hug.

"If I hadn't seen you before you went on, I'd never believe that was your first time," she said, shaking her head. "That was unreal. I'm just glad I don't have to follow you."

Emily drank up the camaraderie, the good wishes and compliments, but her mind was full of Cutter. Should she go out there and find him, or wait and see if he came to her?

"It was way more fun than I thought it would be," she said, trying to keep up her end of the conversation. "I didn't even care that I was naked up there." She paused and looked down at herself. "But now I do. I'd better go get dressed."

She turned around and nearly ran into the manager.

"You're hired," he said without preamble. "I can give you Sunday through Wednesday nights for starters. You'll work six to two and we'll see how it goes."

"Wow, that's great. I mean, thank you."

"Can you do another number tonight?"

"I'm afraid not. Not unless your customers want to see a naked Sleeping Beauty."

"A what?"

"Nothing. I don't have anything else ready, that's all. But I will by tomorrow night."

"Fine, you can go. Just be prepared to dance four times a night from now on."

Smiling to herself, Emily headed back to the dressing room where she sat down and pulled her money out, piling it in her lap. Smoothing out the crumpled bills she counted it, then counted again, hardly able to believe it.

One hundred and fifty three dollars. And she'd only danced once, without even working the floor. This was going to be even more lucrative than she'd expected.

Giddy now, she showered and changed back into her black tank dress and strappy sandals. Her entire body was still buzzing with adrenaline, still awed by what she'd done, and still turned on.

Time to find Cutter.

No one recognized her with her clothes on and makeup off, which was a relief, especially since just being female garnered her more than enough attention. She guzzled a bottle of water and looked around for the man in question. He was taller than just about everyone in the room, so it didn't take long to spot him.

Sadly, her towering self-confidence seemed to be dissipating, and by the time she got within a few feet of him she had no idea what had come over her. First of all, the man was working, secondly, they were in the middle of a crowd of people, and thirdly, she hadn't had a personality transplant, just a temporary blast of endorphins that were rapidly deserting her. She did an about-face and headed for the door.

Then he called her name.

***

Cutter stood near a cluster of tables, keeping an eye on a rowdy bachelor party that seemed just on the verge of getting out of hand, but his head was full of Emily. If it was hard to ignore her before, it was impossible now that he'd seen her strip. She was the sexiest woman he'd ever seen whether she was dressed or undressed. Dressed, it was a restrained kind of sexy that made a man want to set her loose.

Now he knew what she looked like set loose.

He kept reminding himself that he didn't date the dancers, he looked out for them. This new girl certainly didn't need a damn bouncer coming on to her when she was hit on by every man who looked at her. Then again, he could have sworn she was looking at him while she stripped.

He was going back and forth like this in his head when he caught sight of her coming through the crowd of people, turning heads as she went, and damn if she wasn't just as sexy now as she had been on stage. He stood transfixed, his heart rate increasing when it began to look like she might be making her way toward him. He thought she was coming toward him, anyway. Hoped she was, though every instinct told him she was trouble.

She was only a dozen yards away when she looked at him, bit her lip and turned toward the door.

Without even thinking he called out to her.

She stopped where she was, her bare shoulders tensing before she turned around and gave him a tentative smile. Ditching the bachelor party without so much as a glance, he caught up to her, his face breaking into a smile when he got up close. Her black dress clung to her breasts and hips, skimming over those thighs he remembered so well.

She must have guessed what he was thinking, because as he watched, a pink flush rose up her neck and into her cheeks. Was it possible for a woman to blush not an hour after performing the most erotic striptease he'd ever seen?

He ought to say something to put her at ease, let her know he wasn't a total creep.

"You looked good up there."

She looked down at her water bottle as if embarrassed. "Thanks. It felt good to be dancing again. I guess I'm a freak for the stage, because it doesn't seem to matter if I'm performing a gorgeous ballet or taking off my clothes. Weird, huh?"

So she'd been a professional dancer. That explained the moves she laid on Steve.

"I've heard weirder." He paused, wanting to know more about her but not sure she'd want to talk about her past. A lot of the women who worked here didn't. "So why aren't you still dancing?"

Her grip tightened on the bottle and the corners of her mouth turned down. She looked so sad he wished he'd kept his mouth shut.

"I ruptured my Achilles tendon and that was that. My entire career down the drain."

"But you dance just fine. You don't even limp," he said, surprised.

"No, but I can't take the kind of dancing I used to do. Aside from that, the sky's the limit, right? Maybe I'll set Vegas on fire with my pole dancing."

She sounded so bitter and despairing he didn't know what to say. Going from that kind of career to stripping in Vegas was a pretty hard fall.

"I assume Steve hired you?" he asked, changing the subject.

She gave him a wry smile. "Yes. I seem to have won him over despite my less than impressive breast size."

He didn't mean to, he really didn't, but his eyes dropped to her breasts despite what his brain was telling him. Yes, she was small, so small she didn't need a bra, but sleek and perfect, her skin was smooth and white.

He heard her breath catch and came to his senses, looking back up to see her watching him with a flustered, wide-eyed expression. Then she licked her lips, as if nervous, and he damn near lost it.

They stood looking at one another for several long moments, and he could swear she was as aroused and baffled as he was.

Fortunately, though it felt pretty damn *unfortunate*, the hostess hurried over to him.

"I'm really sorry, but there's a seriously drunk guy over at the bar demanding another drink, and Patty's already cut him off. Richie's busy in the VIP room, so..."

She looked at them both apologetically.

"No problem, I'm on it," he said, not sure whether he was relieved or aggravated. He turned back to Emily. "I guess I'll be seeing you."

"Yes. Sure. I'll see you around," she said, smiling uncertainly before heading for the door.

He was definitely in trouble.

Chapter Three

Cutter was heading to the club that Friday morning to work on the expansion of Steve's office when he caught sight of Emily standing on the curb a block away, trying to hail a cab. She raised her hand and waved it around, standing on tiptoe as if the added height would help.

That creamy skin of hers was going to burn if she stood out there much longer. Without planning it he pulled to a stop in front of her and opened the passenger side window.

She'd fallen back a few steps and was frowning and shading her eyes as she looked warily at his truck. Then a smile of recognition spread across her face, lighting her up. Cutter's heart, which had picked up its pace as soon as he saw her, began to pound. He smiled in return, feeling dopey and pleased with how happy she looked to see him.

Which only served to remind him that he shouldn't be going anywhere near her. He'd managed to keep his distance Tuesday and Wednesday and he damn well better keep it now, metaphorically if not literally. He didn't date the dancers. It was a bad idea, not least because he wasn't sure he could handle watching his girl stripping and getting pawed night after night. Watching Emily strip was damn near torture, and he barely even knew her. Maybe that made him some kind of Neanderthal, but it was what it was.

Of course, he didn't have to watch her up there. If he had more control, he'd do his job and keep his eyes on the customers and away from her.

"Need a ride somewhere?" he asked, his annoyance with himself making the question come out more tersely than he'd intended.

Emily approached the truck and peered in the window.

"I need to go get my car from the shop. I don't want to put you out, though."

"You're not. Hop in before you go up in flames, girl."

Emily obeyed, smiling tentatively as she opened the door and climbed onto the high seat. He raised her window and turned the air up to offset the brutal heat. Unfortunately, there wasn't a setting high enough to combat the heat he felt just sitting next to her.

He pulled out into traffic and headed toward the address she gave him, trying to ignore how her pale green sundress had hiked up, revealing a few inches of those killer thighs before she pulled it back down. Seeing her covered up was as erotic as seeing her naked. Regardless, he wasn't going to let on how she affected him. He knew how to play it cool. He wasn't a kid, after all.

He shifted into fifth gear as they hit the highway and glanced over at her. "Still planning on coming back for more next week?" he asked. It was the best he could do, seeing as how he sucked at small talk.

"Definitely. The money's too good to stop now. Besides, I mostly like it. I've been miserable ever since I had to stop dancing. Do you think I'm doing okay though?"

"Well sure, you're doing great. You know, from what I've seen," he added, hoping she hadn't noticed that he'd seen everything.

"I'm used to being critiqued, so it won't bother me if you have pointers. You know, like maybe something I'm doing isn't sexy, that kind of thing. I'm especially concerned about my pole work."

He glanced over at her and couldn't help smiling at the way she was frowning with such seriousness.

"If you got any better at it, you'd probably give everyone in the place a heart attack. Just keep doing what you're doing."

He could feel her looking at him but decided now was a good time to keep his eyes on the road and his thoughts hidden. He'd said quite enough already. A few more minutes passed before she spoke again.

"How long have you been working at the club?"

"About eight months," he answered, knowing she probably wanted him to elaborate. Women always did, but the last thing he wanted was to talk about the slow, painful failure of his business. Besides, if they never got too personal it would be easier to keep some distance between them. Which was why he wasn't asking her any of the questions he had. Like whether she was seeing someone, for instance.

He could sense her watching him, possibly trying to decide whether he was an ass for being so curt, but fortunately they'd arrived at the mechanic's.

"Here we are," he announced, a mixture of regret and relief filling him as she opened the door.

"Great, thanks for the ride," she said, giving him a half-hearted smile as she reached for the door handle. He had the crazy urge to jump out of the truck and run around to open the door for her, as if this were a date. But he certainly hadn't acted like it was a date. He'd barely said five words to the woman.

"You okay getting back?" he asked. "You can follow me if you need to."

"Are you going back to the Strip?"

"Yeah, so it's no problem." This was a flat out lie. He'd been planning to go home, but why tell her that?

Now her smile was full and warm, a shaft of sunlight falling on him. "Thanks, but I think I know the way," she said, hopping down from the seat. "I'll see you Sunday?"

"See you Sunday," he answered, his chest tightening as he watched her walk away.

Two more days and she'd be taking it all off again for a roomful of men. He'd be one of them, watching just as avidly as all those other fools.

***

"Whatever you do, don't date one of the customers. I promise you, it never works out."

It was the beginning of Emily's second week working at the club and Cheryl was filling her in on all the dos and don'ts.

"Not that I have any intention of dating a customer, but why the rule?" Emily asked.

Cheryl sat back and looked at her from under heavily made-up eyes. As far as Emily could tell she didn't put a whole lot of effort into her wardrobe or routine, but she was so sexy and such a good dancer that it didn't seem to matter. The red hair didn't hurt either.

"They'll want you because you seem like the sexiest woman in the world, some kind of lame-o fantasy come to life. But that's all you'll ever be. A guy who meets you here doesn't want to get to know you. He just wants night after night of blow jobs and lap dances."

"Okay, you've convinced me," Emily laughed. She paused a few seconds, not sure if she should ask the next question. "What about the guys who work here? Just for arguments' sake, I could date one of them, right?"

It really shouldn't have mattered, seeing as how she'd only be around for a few weeks, but she hadn't been able to stop thinking of Cutter.

"You mean like the bouncers?"

Emily nodded.

"Sure, knock yourself out. You have your eye on one of them?" Cheryl asked, slanting her a look.

"No," Emily said, maybe a little too quickly. "I was just curious."

"Most of the guys here are decent enough. I went out a few times with Richie, but it didn't amount to anything and we're just friends now. Cutter's the hottest by far and I'm pretty sure he's single, but unfortunately for us he won't date any of the girls. Or maybe it's a good thing, since we'd all be jealous of whoever had rights to that fine bod of his."

"So he doesn't hit on any of the dancers?" Emily asked.

"Nope. Sorry to disappoint you."

"Oh, I didn't mean...I was just curious."

"Alas, he treats us all like we're his little sister."

Emily thought back to the ride in his truck. She'd felt the tension coming off him, and unless she was very much mistaken he was plenty attracted to her. There was nothing sisterly about how he looked at her, but there was definitely something holding him back. She'd wanted to crawl all over that amazing body of his, but everything about his body language had said stay away. He seemed pretty private, and he was a hard man to read.

"I have my own daydreams about him," Cheryl continued. "One day his business is going to pick back up and then he'll be able to quit the club. Maybe after that he'll ditch the big brother act and give me a call."

"What do you mean? Does he own a business?"

"He's a builder. You know, like houses and additions, custom renovations and all that. He had a good thing going and then everything went to hell around here when the economy tanked. He still pulls a few jobs during the day, though."

This explained a lot, and Emily was a bit ashamed that she hadn't thought about his life outside of the club. She'd been too caught up in her overwhelming lust and whether she had the nerve to make a move on him if he didn't hit on her first.

She'd never had casual sex, and her romantic history consisted of exactly two boyfriends. Both those relationships were pretty short-lived and not terribly exciting when it came to the sex. She'd been happy enough to be single, as she'd worked too hard and had too little time for romantic or sexual entanglements.

But things had changed. She had nothing to lose by sowing some wild oats, and she was starting to think a fling with Cutter might be just what she needed. Unfortunately, he wasn't giving her much encouragement. Did she have it in her to throw herself at him if he didn't make a move on her?

"You're the most gorgeous girl here, you know that?"

Emily forced a smile, but Jim was too busy looking at her breasts to notice anyway. "That's sweet of you."

"I'm not just saying that. You're something special, and you dance better than all of them put together."

"Do you live around here, or are you just visiting?" she asked. She could care less where he lived if he was a tourist, but if he lived in the area she'd have to figure out what to do about him. It was only her second Tuesday working there, but he already seemed to know her schedule and had shown up Sunday and Monday as well. Ordinarily she wouldn't have even noticed, since all the guys blended together, but he'd been monopolizing her attention. Every time she came out onto the floor he called her over and kept her talking, holding her wrist with a creepy possessiveness.

"I live here," he said. "Got a good job working for the city."

"Oh, that's great," Emily replied, just barely covering her dismay.

"How about I take you out sometime? You're off Thursday, right?"

Even if Cheryl hadn't given her the talk about not dating customers, she would have had no hesitation in declining Jim's invitation.

"I'm sorry, I can't. I'm seeing someone."

"Is that so?" he said, a hard edge to his voice.

Emily froze, unsure what would have made him suspicious. A few men had already asked her out and she had her answer down pat, no hesitation whatsoever. Then again, maybe he was just damaged and suspicious of everyone.

"Sorry," she said, determined to put more distance between them from now on. No money was worth his creepiness.

She turned to go, only to be brought up short by his hand on her wrist. A flutter of panic started in her chest and she wondered if she'd have to call for help. Then she caught sight of Cutter watching from about twenty feet away, ready to move if she gave him the go-ahead.

"I really need to get going," she said, striving for civility.

"What's your rush? Give me a lap dance and I'll make it worth your while," Jim said, his tone demanding, his expression even more unnerving than before. It wasn't the dumb-ass look most drunk, horny guys had when they asked. This was belligerent and vaguely threatening.

"Sorry, I don't do those," she said, trying again to pull away.

But instead of letting go he pulled harder, catching her off-balance so that she fell across his lap. Helplessness poured through her at the feel of his erection pressing into her hip, his hands holding her to him. But it was only for a matter of seconds and then Cutter was there, looming over them, his expression beyond furious. He put his hand to the back of Jim's neck and did some sort of martial art, ninja thing and Jim instantly let go, his whole body going slack.

Emily scrambled off, shivering in disgust and faintly nauseated.

"Are you okay?" Cutter asked, his voice low, and she nodded. "Why don't you take a break. I'll deal with this guy."

"Thanks," she said, her smile turning wobbly as tears threatened.

Cutter looked torn, like he didn't know whether he should keep hold of Jim, who was starting to squirm, or attend to her. She ought to get out of the way and let him handle things. Besides, he was right, she did need to take a break before she lost it in front of everyone. So far they hadn't made much of a scene and she wanted to keep it that way.

In the dressing room she put on her robe and paced the room, too agitated to sit. She felt dirty, violated really, though no real harm had been done. But her sexy little adventure was showing its dark side, one she'd been willfully ignoring. You could shake your tits and ass in a roomful of men for only so long before one of them was going to get out of line. She just hadn't expected it to happen to her.

She spent a few minutes doing her barre warm-up and before long she felt calmer, more centered. A few of the girls came in and asked how she was doing and before long they were telling their own stories of troublesome customers. The fact that every single woman had had at least one disturbing encounter was sobering, but the camaraderie brought its own comfort.

She danced two more times, but she was just going through the motions without any of the usual pleasure she took when she danced. Luckily no one seemed to notice. The flirtatious chitchat as she worked the floor was even harder, but since that was where she made about half her tips she pushed on.

By the time her shift was over she was exhausted. Compared to the rigors of performing a full-length ballet, dancing here was usually a cake-walk, but the scene with Jim had taken its toll. If she hadn't made over five hundred dollars tonight, she might have considered bagging the whole enterprise. But her credit card payments wouldn't be improved by her delicate sensibilities.

It was a relief to shower away her stripper identity and change back into an innocuous wraparound skirt and sleeveless top. Cutter was embroiled in what looked like a heated discussion at the bar, so she continued out the door. She'd thank him properly tomorrow.

Outside people walked around with the usual neon-lit energy, and the hotel was nearly as busy at two-thirty in the morning as it had been early in the evening. A wall separated the bank of elevators from the lobby, and it was blessedly peaceful. The few other people waiting got on the elevator for the lower floors and it was just her.

Finally her elevator arrived and she got on, only vaguely aware of someone else behind her. She was digging around in her bag for her key card, annoyed with herself for not having it out, when someone grabbed her arm.

Startled, she looked up to find Jim standing beside her.

Emily's blood ran cold and for a few seconds her brain froze, unable to process what was happening.

"Not so sure of yourself now, are you?" he said, his eyes burning with malice.

Now that he wasn't sitting down she realized how tall he was, far taller than she. Full-blown panic set in and she threw herself forward, trying to push past him. With an almost casual shove he tossed her back against the wall, knocking the breath out of her so that even her cry for help came out a pitiful croak.

She watched the doors close with rising terror. But just before they shut she caught sight of Cutter running toward her, calling her name.

"What's your room number?" Jim demanded, the question so ludicrous Emily could only stare at him.

With a snarl at her he began pressing all the buttons, his frustration growing as they remained stubbornly un-lit, the elevator sitting on the lobby floor. Emily watched, almost of if she weren't part of the unfolding scene, curious how long it would take him to figure out that a key card was needed to operate the elevator.

Her mind raced, inventorying her bag, considering each item and its possibilities as a weapon. Her stiletto heels were back in her locker, as was her hairspray. She had precious little with which to fend him off, but that didn't mean she wasn't going to try. Anyway, he couldn't keep her in the elevator forever, and surely Cutter would take care of him after that.

No sooner did she have this thought than the doors opened again with an innocent ding. Cutter stood there blocking the doorway, every muscle tensed and waiting, his dark eyes looking almost crazed with fear and fury.

Jim took a step backwards but there was nowhere to go. With a low growl Cutter hauled him out of the elevator, one precise punch to the gut doubling him over. Cutter shoved him down onto his knees, twisting his arms behind him.

A man and woman in evening dress come around the corner just then, stopping in shock at the bizarre scene. As bad as it looked, however, it was clear that Cutter had everything under control. In fact he was managing Jim's bulk easily. He looked like he wanted to kill the man rather than subdue him, but so far he was restraining himself admirably.

Things had taken on a surreal aspect, but Emily roused herself to go find a security guard. She found two on the other side of the lobby and returned with them to find that a small crowd had formed around Jim and Cutter. Emily relaxed somewhat as the guards took control, ignoring Jim's rants about Cutter jumping him.

"I'm sure you'll see all you need to know on the security cameras," Cutter said as he and Emily gave their contact information.

"What's the big deal?" Jim yelled, struggling against the guard who held him. "She's just a stripper for God's sake."

Emily blanched, mortified, and felt Cutter's arm go around her.

Soon a couple of police officers arrived and Emily sat down on a chair to fill out a report.

Finally, after profuse apologies from the manager on duty and assurances that her assailant wouldn't be allowed to enter the hotel ever again, Cutter took Emily's arm and led her to the elevator. They rode the twenty-two floors in silence, though she could feel the tension radiating off him. Even so, just his presence comforted her no end.

They reached her room and stood awkwardly outside her door.

"Would you mind coming in for a little while?" she asked, hating how vulnerable she sounded.

"Oh, you mean you're staying here?" he asked, looking relieved.

Emily frowned in confusion. "Yes, what did you think I was doing?"

"I guess I thought maybe you were coming to see a guest. Like, a man."

"God, no." she said, horrified by the thought of him walking her to the door, all the while thinking he was delivering her to some man's arms. "I'm just...I'm staying here." She let out a sigh. Might as well tell him the whole truth. "I'm not planning on being around long enough to need a place to live."

"Oh. I see," he said, though she could tell he didn't. How could he?

His expression had closed off, like he wasn't going to give anything away. She unlocked the door and stepped inside, hoping he wasn't going to change his mind about staying. She breathed a sigh of relief when he followed her in and shut the door.

Emily set her bag on the dresser and kicked off her shoes, unsure what to do now that they were inside.

"Would you like something to drink?" she asked. "I'm afraid all I have is grapefruit juice or bottled water."

"Water would be great."

Emily grabbed a couple of waters from the little fridge and sat down on the loveseat, then held her breath as she waited to see if Cutter would sit next to her or on the armchair. She let out her breath as he sat next to her, though it wasn't exactly relief. She was suddenly all too aware of how often in the past week she'd imagined him in the enormous bed just a few yards away.

Her face heated at the thought and she looked down at the bottle in her hand, willing herself to act like a normal person.

"I wanted to thank you before I left the club tonight, but you were busy. Now I have a whole lot more to thank you for."

Cutter sat forward, his hands on his knees, as if ready to spring out of his seat.

"You don't need to thank me. The last thing I'd do is let someone hurt you."

She felt her throat grow tight and fought to keep her breathing regular. It took a few moments before she trusted herself to speak.

"So how exactly did you happen to be right outside the elevators when I needed you?"

He shrugged his shoulders, looking embarrassed. "I wanted to see if you were okay, but you left before I got a chance. I stuck my head out and saw you heading into the hotel and followed you. I guess you didn't hear me calling. I kind of felt like a stalker until I saw that bastard shove you."

His voice was rough with emotion and his eyes held a whole world of doubt and resistance that she didn't understand. But she wanted to, wanted to find a way through it. Wanted to run her hands along that smooth dark skin, those hard muscles he was so willing to use on her behalf.

"I don't know what would have happened if you hadn't come along, but I do know tonight could have been a lot nastier."

"I just wish I'd gotten there quicker. When those doors closed on you..."

"As soon as I saw you I knew I'd be okay."

A ragged breath tore from his throat and heat flared in his eyes. Then they were both moving, coming together without another word. Emily heard herself moan, the tension of the entire night igniting as his mouth covered hers, hungry and demanding.

One big hand cupped the back of her head, the other curved around her hip, holding her to him so that her breasts pressed against his hard chest, abrading her already sensitive nipples. Her hands dove into his hair, held his face in her hands, kissing him in an effort to put out the fire they'd started and scorching herself in the process.

His tongue sought her out, stroking her from every angle, first shallow and then deeper until she was boneless. He kissed her as if he'd never stop, as if it were all he needed until the end of time. She drank up his urgency and matched it with her own, crawling into his lap to be closer. The heat and scent of him enveloped her, his strong thighs beneath her, his arousal pressing against her through her underwear. All her senses were full of him, her body swept through by its own restless cravings.

His hand left her hip to cup her breast, a ragged groan coming from low in his throat as she whimpered against him. She was panting now, desperate for him, her mouth traveling down his throat, nipping as she went, loving the sounds she pulled from him.

Then a cell phone rang, its shrill noise ripping through the room.

Emily jumped, startled, and slid off him so he could dig the phone out of his back pocket. Cutter looked at the phone and grimaced.

"Fuck. It's my sister. I forgot I was supposed to pick her up after her shift."

His head fell back onto the sofa and he closed his eyes. After a few seconds of heaving breaths he sat up and looked at her, his expression wiped clean of all desire and need. A dismay so profound it was more akin to grief washed over her at the look of resolve on his face. She watched, incredulous, as he stood up.

How could he go from the torrid kisses of a minute ago to this dispassionate stranger? Her entire body was still throbbing with need.

"Maybe it's for the best," he said, shoving his hands into the pockets of his black dress pants. "I should never have let things get so out of hand, not when you were so shaken up."

"Cutter, we didn't do anything I didn't want to do. I'm a grown woman and I know what I want."

A muscle in his jaw twitched and his eyes flared before he tamped down whatever feeling he'd been about to betray.

"I just think it would be better if we don't get involved."

"Because you have some kind of policy against dating dancers?"

"I wouldn't exactly call it a policy..."

"Never mind. I get it."

She really didn't get it, but she wasn't going to let him know how let down she was. She stood up and followed him to the door.

"Well, thanks for everything," she said, hating how inane it sounded.

"Emily –"

She looked at him expectantly.

He hesitated and then shook his head, and whatever he'd been about to say was lost to her. "Sleep well."

"You bet," she said, and watched him walk down the hallway, an ache squeezing her chest as she shut the door.

Chapter Four

Cutter pulled up in front of the restaurant where Lisa worked and waited as she climbed in.

"You're late," she said without preamble.

"Yeah, I know. Sorry," he said, knowing he sounded short but unable to help it.

"What's with you?" she asked. "I'm the one who's supposed to be annoyed."

He took a deep breath and tried to release some of the tension that had been with him since leaving Emily. If only he could stop smelling her hair and remembering how soft her skin was, not to mention the look on her face when he walked out on her.

"It was just a crazy night, that's all. Some guy went all stalker on one of the dancers and attacked her in a hotel elevator."

"Jeez, that's insane. What did it have to do with you, though?"

"I saw him do it and took the bastard down. It felt damn good, too," he said, immediately realizing he'd raised more questions than he'd answered.

"Okay, spill it. I want full, complex sentences, Cutter. Why exactly were you with this woman in a hotel? You have a lady friend you haven't told me about?"

Christ. He shouldn't have said anything. Lisa never let things go.

"It's not like that. Maybe I am attracted to her, but it doesn't matter. I never date the dancers."

"And why exactly is that?" Lisa asked, an edge to her voice.

He had to tread carefully here. "A lot of reasons, okay? But I don't feel like explaining myself to you."

"I hope this isn't about what happened to me," Lisa said. "Not everyone is stripping for drug money, you know. If you don't want to get involved with someone who's got problems, fine. I just hope you aren't throwing down roadblocks out of some misguided sense of honor. Frankly, if I was one of those dancers, I'd be offended by your patronizing attitude."

"Excuse me?" he said, incredulous.

"You heard me. Not every stripper is as screwed up as I was. And you're not responsible for saving them even if they are. Anyway, for all you know, the woman you like has her shit way more together than you do."

"Well that wouldn't be hard, would it?" he snapped.

"I didn't mean –"

"Maybe you didn't, but you're right. I have nothing to offer. Just ask Amy."

"I never liked Amy, and as far I'm concerned you're better off without her." Lisa was in full righteous sister mode now. "What kind of woman leaves a guy just because things aren't perfect anymore?"

"Just forget it, okay?"

They'd reached her apartment complex, but she remained in her seat and he could feel her eyes on him.

"You're such a great guy, Cutter," she said, her voice quiet. "I just wish you'd let someone take care of *you* for a change."

A wave of tenderness washed over him as he looked at Lisa's earnest expression. He sighed, all of his anger draining away. "I'll think about it. Now get inside. It's late."

He watched as she dug in her bag for her keys and then let herself in. Not until she'd waved from inside did he pull away.

He spent the whole drive home examining his actions and motivations, wondering if he had some sort of complex. But it wasn't like he was some martyr pining for the dancers and denying himself anyway. He really did want to look out for them the way he wished someone had done for Lisa. No one had tempted him in all this time, maybe because a lot of them had some complicated shit going on in their lives, but also because he'd been kind off women since Amy.

Then Emily came along.

The first time he saw her he'd felt like he had as a teenager, watching the blond girls at school like they were exotic animals. Which they were to him. He'd just switched high schools to live with his father, and it was his first time going to school off the reservation. He'd felt like an alien and was sure he'd never make friends.

He used to try to imagine what their lives were like, their houses and bedrooms, but he came up completely empty. He knew one thing, though. They weren't in run-down shacks on land so barren and undesirable the government happily gave it to the Washoe.

It had been ages since he'd thought about high school, and lord knew he'd slept with enough blonds since then. But Emily pushed his buttons for some reason. He felt a touch of what he had as a teenager when he was around her, like she was part of another world and maybe he'd get a taste but he couldn't really have her. Now that they'd kissed, it was even worse.

If she hadn't confessed that she'd be leaving soon, he'd probably be on his way back to her hotel room right now. But he already liked her way more than he should for something that could only be brief and casual. The last thing he wanted was to be some guy she slummed with during her adventure in Las Vegas.

So maybe it was his protective instinct that was getting in the way, only it wasn't like Lisa thought. This time it was himself he was protecting.

***

Emily swatted desperately at her alarm the next morning, groaning with fatigue, only to realize the sound that woke her was her phone ringing.

"Hello?" she croaked, sounding like she'd smoked several packs of cigarettes.

"Did I wake you, honey? I'm sorry. I was sure you'd be up by now."

It was ten o'clock, the usual time she got up now that she worked so late, though her mother assumed she still got up early like most working adults. She'd tossed and turned all night, her thoughts stuck on Cutter, so even the late hour hadn't left her rested.

She sat up and tried to clear her head.

"It's fine, Mom," she said, forcing cheer into her voice. "I guess I just overslept. What's up?"

"Not too much. I hadn't heard from you for a few days so I wanted to see how the ballet is coming along."

She'd told her mother she was working with the Nevada Ballet Theater on the staging of a ballet she'd once starred in. Now every time she talked to her it meant telling more lies, so she'd been avoiding it. Which wasn't fair and only ratcheted up her daily dose of guilt.

"It's going great. They seem to like what I'm contributing."

"That's great, honey."

They talked for a few more minutes before Emily hung up, relieved her mom didn't ask too many questions. The money was really going to come in handy, but she didn't want her mom to know just how much she needed it, or what she was doing to get it.

Forcing herself out of bed, she started a pot of coffee and ate a protein bar. As soon as the caffeine had taken hold she dressed in her old practice clothes and headed for the club. Steve had agreed to let her practice when the club was closed, as she wasn't in anyone's way. There was always someone else there – the janitor, the bookkeeper, a vendor trying to work out a deal with Steve – but she had the stage to herself and no one bothered her while she practiced her pole work or worked out the choreography for her routines.

First she went through an abbreviated version of what she'd have done in company class if she were still there, taking care not to do anything that would tax her injured foot. When she was properly warmed up she went through all four dances she'd be doing that night, refining her moves as she went.

It was her version of a dress rehearsal, complete with the tunes she'd chosen playing softly on the sound system. Maybe it was overkill, but if she was going to dance naked in front of hundreds of people, then she was damn well going to be prepared. She wasn't going to take anything for granted, even if all anyone cared about was seeing her naked. Unlike a ballet audience, the customers at the club were right there, their faces visible. As intimidating as that was, it was kind of cool, too. Dance could bring tears to a person's eyes or it could make a man hard. Either way she was reaching them.

Since she had no friends and no life outside of the club she spent all her free time working on her performances, as well as on a dance she was tentatively beginning to choreograph. It was an idea she'd had before her injury, only then she'd had no time, nor any reason, to pursue it.

Maybe she was trying to replicate the structure of her days with the company – warm-up and class in the morning, rehearsals in the afternoons. Then again, it was all she knew, and at least it gave her days some focus, two things she'd been sorely lacking of late. It was a fragile lifeline, and one she held onto, as she was by no means reconciled to her new situation. She'd once been part of something bigger than herself. Now she felt like she'd been excommunicated and thrown out into the cold.

After a couple hours she headed back to her room to change and shower and call a couple of friends who'd left messages. All of her friends were ballet dancers, and she'd had enough pity from them already, so she told them she was hanging in Vegas with a friend from high school and sightseeing for a week or two. More lies, but there was no way was she telling anyone she was stripping. It would sound even worse than it was and she'd end up some kind of cautionary tale for dancers with weak ankles.

Relieved to hang up after the last call, she settled down to work on some costumes with the TV on for company. Just before six she headed back to the club, relieved that Cutter didn't work Wednesdays. It would spare them both the awkwardness, at least for the night.

Her shift went by without anything out of the ordinary happening, but as the night wore on she grew more and more nervous. What if Jim was lurking somewhere between the club and the hotel? Or what if he somehow managed to get into the hotel and attack her again?

She was probably just being paranoid. The streets were always full of people when she got off her shift, and it was a short walk back to the hotel. She needed to suck it up or she'd be scared every night.

But logic only went so far. She dawdled in the dressing room talking to some of the dancers, and took her time in the shower, washing her hair and shaving her legs. Then, still not quite ready to leave, she sorted and organized the clothes and props in her locker. When she could think of nothing else to do, she finally threw everything in her bag, took a deep breath and headed out onto the floor.

She was almost at the door when she heard someone calling her name and Richie came up beside her.

"Hang on, I'll walk you home."

She stared at him, thrilled at the offer but totally taken by surprise. By now everyone had heard about Jim attacking her last night, but even so she and Richie didn't do much more than say hi to one another.

"Are you sure? I don't want to put you out or anything."

"It's no problem. Brian's covering for me."

Her relief was so immense she realized how scared she'd really been. Richie held the door open for her and followed her out, his hands shoved in his pockets and his eyes watchful.

"I really appreciate you doing this," she said.

"I'm happy to do it, but I can't take all the credit. Cutter called me earlier today and asked if I'd see you back to your room. Once he told me what had happened I figured it was the least I could do."

Emily stopped mid-stride, floored that Cutter had arranged this for her. Even when he was nowhere around he was looking out for her. How was she going to get over the man when he did things like this?

Richie waited for her to catch up. "I know, what a mensch, right?" He shook his head as if baffled himself. "I can't say I have him figured out, but he's a good guy."

Emily laughed, charmed by his lighthearted manner. He wasn't as handsome as Cutter, but there was something sweet and comforting about him at the moment. It was a far cry from his bouncer persona and it left her thinking about how changeable people were. Some people more than others.

***

"Thanks for asking Richie to walk me home the other night."

Cutter shrugged, his hands going to his pockets. "I just thought you might be nervous."

"You were right, I was," she said, watching the play of emotions cross Cutter's face. Concern, discomfort, embarrassment. Why did he make everything so complicated?

They were standing in the back hallway, not far from the VIP room. Emily was in full costume, though *full* probably wasn't the most accurate description of it, seeing as how her first performance tonight would be as Salomé. She'd choreographed her own striptease version of the dance of the seven veils, throwing in a few moves inspired by the Salomé ballet she once danced.

She could see Cutter making an effort to keep his eyes trained on her face, and it made her feel just a little better that the transparent, jewel-colored scarves drifting around her were proving to be such a distraction. Maybe he wasn't as in control as he seemed.

"Is there a problem, here?" Steve asked, coming toward them down the hallway, his habitual scowl firmly in place.

"No, no problem," Cutter replied, looking a touch guilty. "I was just heading onto the floor."

Cutter walked away and Steve looked Emily up and down. "Nice, babe. They're gonna love it."

And they did love it. It was her best performance so far, certainly her most creative, and she even did it to instrumental music with a lot of sitar and exotic flair. One by one she sent each veil drifting down to the stage, the men watching her like she was the sexist woman on earth. And she felt like it, too. She was a woman out of mythology, a biblical seductress come to life to mesmerize her followers. Her body floated through the air, and she could almost smell the incense burning, feel the hot wind.

Then she looked out into the audience and there was Cutter, caught up in her spell. following every move like she knew he would be.

By the time she came off stage she was as aroused as the audience, her mind full of Cutter and their wild kiss.

But she couldn't get near him. He kept his distance the rest of the night, paying attention to her only when she was onstage. She knew him well enough by now to understand that he watched her reluctantly, against his will. Which meant he felt something for her and was trying to deny it. But why?

She walked offstage after her third striptease, emptied her money into her locker, and headed back out to work the floor, her engines revving. Between stripping and watching Cutter without being able to touch him, she was feeling dangerous.

She strolled around the room, leaning closer to the patrons than usual, touching an arm, throwing her head back and laughing at every effort to amuse her. Another girl started dancing to "Some Girls," a naughty and politically incorrect song that only made her hotter.

Then she spotted Cutter sitting at a table talking to two other men. The way they were laughing, it looked like he probably knew them. Maybe he was on break, though he didn't usually hang out in the audience.

God, he was gorgeous. His long legs were stretched out alongside the table, a muscled arm hooked over the side of the chair. He could have been a model, one of those men gazing out of magazines and making every other man you saw look bad. Except he was right here, and she knew his kisses were fierce and hot and unbelievably sexy.

She walked over to his table and stood smiling at the two men seated with him.

"Would you two fellas like to buy your friend here a lap dance? He looks like he could use a little fun."

The two guys looked at each other and grinned, but Cutter sat up and stared at her. "What are you talking about? You never do lap dances."

"Hell yeah, we'll pay for a lap dance, honey," his friend said. "Make it a good one. Cutter here takes things too seriously."

Cutter started to get up, but she was through letting him walk away. One hand on his shoulder to keep him in place, she leaned down and whispered in his ear. "Don't worry. This won't hurt a bit."

*****

Cutter didn't know if he was in heaven or hell. His mind seemed to freeze as Emily let out a husky laugh and swung one long, bare leg over his lap and her sweet ass settled right on his cock, which had already grown hard. Then again, he'd pretty much been hard since he met her. His hands automatically went to her hips, whether to hold her to him or push her away, he had no idea.

Her skin shimmered in the lights, so pale next to his own. His hands were moving over her, restless to feel every inch of her. She smiled a wicked smile and then arched her back, thrusting her perfect little breasts up until it was all he could do not to bend over and take one in his mouth.

He knew better than anyone what the rules for lap dances were, and he was already breaking them. But she wanted him to, he could feel it. She was taunting him, trying to get him to react.

She rose up until her breasts were only a few inches from his mouth, then sank back down, letting them brush against his chest. Then she began riding him in earnest, teasing his cock with every x-rated move. She was like a lioness he'd watched on one of those nature shows. Fierce but relaxed and totally in control as she went in for the kill. Within a minute he was painfully hard, desperate to enter her and furious that she'd driven him to the edge in a public place.

He grabbed her arms and pushed her back until she looked at him, her eyes heavy and dazed with desire.

She wasn't playing with him. This is what she'd looked like that night in her room, right before the damn phone had rung. It took her a few seconds to focus, but whatever she saw in his expression startled her. In one smooth motion she slipped off his lap.

Frank and Scott looked between him and Emily with confusion. Then Frank smiled and held out a fifty-dollar bill. Emily shook her head and took a step back.

"That one was on the house," she said, her voice shaky. Then she turned and walked away without looking back.

"Holy shit, dude. What was that?" Scott asked.

"I'm not sure, but I'm sure as hell going to find out."

Blood pumping madly through his veins, he strode across the room. It was all he could do not to break out in a run. Furious, aroused and confused, he headed straight for the dressing room. Emily was just tying the belt on her silky blue robe when he got there. She raised a brow at him but didn't say a word.

Two other women were in there getting ready.

"Hey sweetie, you need something?" Cheryl asked.

"I just need to talk to Emily for a second," he said, trying to sound causal.

He smiled tightly, hoping no one noticed his throbbing hard-on.

"Go on, Emily. Don't keep the man waiting," Cheryl said, giving Emily a little push toward him.

Cutter let her precede him out of the room, ignoring the avid looks from the other women. Out in the hallway he urged her forward until they reached a closed door.

"In here," he ordered, reaching around her to open the supply closet.

She looked up at him, hesitating as if she'd lost whatever nerve she'd had, but he wasn't backing down. Finally she relented and walked inside.

He closed the door behind them and locked it.

"You want to tell me what that was all about?" he asked, moving toward her until her back was against the door. But even as he asked, another part of his brain answered: *Who cares?*

She was still in her fuck-me heels, but even so he was a good six inches taller than her. He pushed her long, silken hair off her shoulder and smoothed his palm over her skin, unable to keep from touching her. She trembled and a pulse throbbed in her neck.

She looked up at him, her lush mouth set in a stubborn pout, her eyes defiant and uncertain. "Maybe I wanted you to see what you were missing."

"You're killing me, Emily," he said, his voice coming out rough and desperate.

But he was done talking, done caring about the fallout. He wanted her now.

His mouth slanted down over hers, the first taste of her nearly bringing him to his knees. She opened for him immediately, her whimper of need driving him even more insane. Kissing her was like drinking from a well in the desert, and he couldn't stop. Her lips were soft, her mouth tasting faintly of red wine, and he dove into her again and again, his tongue dancing with hers, insistent and demanding.

She molded herself to him without hesitation, her robe falling open so that he could feel the heat of her bare breasts and thighs. He pressed himself to her, letting her feel his full arousal, driving himself crazy. Her hands ran over him, restlessly touching everywhere, sliding under his shirt where her nails dug into him, urging him on.

He was so far gone, all he could think about was pulling his cock out and driving into her, making her call his name, feeling her tight heat around him. The need was so desperate and real he pulled back, closing his eyes as he tried to gain some semblance of control.

Chapter Five

Emily's eyes drifted open and she looked dazedly at Cutter, still in her arms but now pulled slightly back, his face tense with need and restraint.

"Why did you stop?" she asked, her voice coming out husky and full of naked desire.

She no longer cared.

"I'm trying not to act like a damn animal."

"Maybe I want you to," you said, her fingernails raking his back, pulling him to her, offering herself to him without reservation.

It was as if she'd raised the door of a cage. His eyes darkened and he looked at her for the space of a heartbeat. Then his mouth took hers again, his tongue filling her, demanding everything she had. Her legs trembled and her clit swelled and throbbed, the thin strip of her thong abrading her into a near frenzy.

A moment later she felt his hands at her shoulders and then the silken whisper as her robe pooled at her feet. He groaned her name, his voice low and rough as his hands cupped her breasts, toying with the tight buds. His hands were big and calloused, a workingman's hands, and they roamed over every inch of her feverish skin. His breath was ragged as he ran a hand over her hip to her thigh, sliding his fingers beneath the tight band of her garter.

She needed to feel him. Her fingers trembled as they worked at the buttons of his shirt, slowing her down until she groaned in frustration. Cutter let out a husky laugh and pulled the shirt over his head, tossing it to the floor. She rested her palms on his chest, holding him still so that she could look her fill.

The only light came from the neon signs outside the high window, but even so she could see the contours of his muscles. His chest was smooth and perfectly defined, an artist's rendering of what a man should be. Needing to explore him, to make him hers, she ran her hands over his chest and stomach, lingering on the fine ridges of muscle above his pants. Bolder now, she pressed her hand against the huge bulge straining against his zipper, smiling with satisfaction at his pained groan.

But even that wasn't enough. She was aching for him, hollow with need as she worked franticly to get her hands on him. She listened to the delicious sound of his labored breathing as she released his huge erection, running her hand up and down in pure feminine approval. He tried to press her back against the wall, but she eluded him, dropping to the floor to take him in her mouth.

Never had she felt so carnal, so desperate to take everything a man had to offer, to give him every kind of pleasure. She knelt on her robe and took him into her mouth, the tension in him nearly singing as she sucked him.

His hands went rigid in her hair as she played with him, using her hand in time with her mouth. As powerful and in control as he usually was, she made him tremble and pant her name right alongside God's. Her own excitement rose alongside his, everything in her alive to his warm skin and thrashing pulse.

Then he pulled her up, his hands fisting in her hair as he tipped her head back to receive his desperate, almost painful kiss. His hand covered her pussy, pulling a long moan out of her. She clutched his arms to keep from melting to the floor as one strong finger slipped beneath her thong and stroked until she was writhing against him. His mouth left hers to close over a nipple, sucking and lightly biting as his fingers slid into her, again and again.

"You're so wet," he groaned, his voice raw.

"Please, Cutter," she said, nearly sobbing with need.

He leaned his forehead against hers as his breath heaved in and out. "I don't have any protection."

"It's a strip club," Emily said, half crazed with desperation. "There have to be condoms somewhere. What about the men's bathroom?"

"Right. Wait here while I –"

"Cutter, look behind you," she said, pointing to a box on the shelf behind him. It was a supply closet after all, and they now had at their disposal the biggest box of condoms she'd ever laid eyes on.

"Praise Jesus," he breathed, pulling the box down.

He took a packet out and ripped it with his teeth while Emily stroked him, desperate to get him inside her.

He sheathed himself and then his hands were under her ass, easily lifting her up and pressing her back against the wall.

"You want this, Emily?" he asked, his expression fierce, his face taut as he held himself in check.

"God, yes," she gasped, wrapping her legs around his waist and gripping his shoulders.

Without another word he pulled her thong aside, entering her in one tortuously slow stroke. Her head fell back and she arched in pure ecstasy, taking him in as deep as he'd go.

"You feel amazing. So tight," he said, his praise given between ragged breaths.

Her fingers dug deeper into his shoulders with each powerful thrust as he drove into her, hitting her sweet spot until she could hardly bear it. He filled her exquisitely, the tension coiling tighter and tighter until she was sobbing with need.

"You want to come, baby?" he asked.

Wordlessly she nodded, too far gone for speech, the feel of him between her splayed legs beyond anything she'd ever known.

"Touch yourself," he whispered in her ear, his voice a dark seduction.

She looked at him uncertainly.

"Go on, show me how you do it.

He watched as she took one hand from his shoulder and brought it between them to stroke her painfully throbbing clit. He stayed with her, keeping her pace, thrusting in time with her rhythm until she didn't know where he ended and she began. They were just bodies coming together as if they'd been made for each other, their skin slick with sweat.

Sensation built until it was nearly unbearable, her thoughts narrowing to the vortex of pleasure pulling her under. She hovered on the peak for endless seconds and then broke around him with such violence he had to hold her to him. She was still drifting back down when he spread her legs wider and thrust home, burying his face in her neck as his cock pulsed inside her and his big body shook in release.

Her eyes were still closed, her body boneless, but Cutter had hold of her. His face was still buried in her neck, his cock still inside her. Their hearts beat almost in time, slowing down as the seconds passed. She wanted just a few more minutes breathing in the glorious scents of sex and sweat, a musky combination that should have been indecent. A few more minutes of this intimate, hard-won knowledge of how he felt and looked and sounded.

He drew back and carefully pulled out of her, making sure the condom didn't fall off, and Emily lowered her feet to the floor. She stared at his chest, wondering what she'd find when she looked him in the eye, terrified he'd want to pretend none of this had ever happened.

Then the doorknob rattled as someone tried to get in.

She and Cutter looked at each other, panicked, as Stan swore on the other side of the door. They stood, barely breathing, until he walked away.

"We have to get out of here. He'll probably be back with a key in a matter of minutes," Cutter said, bending down to retrieve her robe. He held it for her as if he were helping her into her coat. "You go first."

"But what about you?" she asked.

He was bare-chested, his pants down around his chiseled hips. A delectable sight, and one that brought a smile to her lips. Still, she didn't want anyone else finding him in this state.

He looked down at himself and smiled ruefully. "Don't worry, I'll be dressed in two seconds," he said, retrieving his shirt from where it hung over a cardboard box.

Unlocking the door, he stuck his head out and looked around.

"The coast is clear," he said, grinning wolfishly at her as he held the door open just enough for her to squeeze through.

Emily stumbled into the hallway, her legs still weak and trembling. Smoothing her hair back, she pulled her robe more tightly around her and headed for the dressing room. She had to go on once more tonight, and she had a feeling she didn't have much time to get ready.

She heard Stan whistling from around the corner and looked back, relieved to see Cutter coming out of the storage closet, his clothes once again intact. His hair was tousled and his color high, but no one would think much of that. His gaze raked her from the tip of her spiked heels on up. His eyes met hers and a slow, devastating smile spread across his face. Then turned and headed onto the floor.

She was still standing there, breathless, when Stan walked by, key in hand, and opened the closet door.

Hurrying now, she entered the dressing room and looked at the time. Twelve-thirty. She'd have to hurry to get ready. Unfortunately, Cheryl had just finished her set and was busy fixing her make-up.

"I guess there's something between you after all," she said, turning from the mirror and fixing Emily with a look.

"There wasn't when we last talked about it. But yes, there is, though I don't know what you'd call it."

"Don't you?" Cheryl replied, her voice tinged with bitterness.

"I'm really sorry, Cheryl. I guess I should have realized you'd be upset. It just all happened so fast..."

"Forget it." Cheryl sighed and gave a wan smile. "I had no claim on him. I'm just surprised is all. I'll get over it. I just hope you know how lucky you are."

Emily's mouth opened but she was at a loss for words.

Cheryl laughed. "Hurry up, sweetie, you're on in ten minutes.

Relieved that Cheryl didn't hate her, Emily pulled out the costume for her next set and took stock of her appearance. Wild hair, flushed face, swollen lips. Pretty much the look strippers strove for, only she'd come by hers honestly. Hopefully only Cheryl would know that, though.

She worked to keep herself from acting too dreamy as she got ready and made sure to stop any goofy smiles before they escaped. Other dancers filtered in and out with none of them seeming any the wiser and she wanted to keep in that way. Especially since she didn't know what any of it meant. Would it be the first and last time she and Cutter had sex, or could she look forward to more?

She wasn't sure how she could stand being around him if he rejected her now. It was bad enough before she knew what sort of magic he was capable of. As high as her expectations had been, he'd blown them out of the water. Just thinking about what he'd done to her made her hot all over again.

But enough speculating. She'd find out soon enough what he wanted. Right now she had to get ready for another striptease. If history was anything to go by, she could count on Cutter watching her just as avidly as he always did.

***

Cutter moved around the room, his eyes scanning the crowd but only half seeing it. How was he supposed to think of anything but Emily? He could still smell her skin, feel the wet heat of her mouth on him, her legs wrapped around his waist as he plunged into her, more out of control than he'd been since he was a teenager.

He only hoped it wasn't a one-time deal. Now that he knew what he'd been missing, nothing on earth was going to keep him away from her if she was still willing. His cock throbbed again, threatening to come back to life. He had to take his mind off of Emily or he'd be damned uncomfortable the rest of the night.

Then Emily strode out on stage to the tune of Janis Joplin's "Piece of My Heart" and once again he was nailed to the floor, riveted on Emily and good for nothing except lusting after her. She was dressed the way a woman might have been in the late sixties - skimpy tank top and no bra, a long, filmy skirt through which you could see her legs. Her hair was loose and messy. Messy from their wild fucking, a thought that made him want to charge the stage and drag her off. She danced as if losing herself at a concert, one where everyone was shedding their clothes in an orgy of ecstasy.

Christ, she was good. Looking around, it was clear everyone else thought so, too. Part of him was proud of her dancing, her unerring sense of how to make a dance work with a particular song so that each one was an experience in and of itself. But he had to work to control the possessiveness that made him want to shield her from all those stares. He knew exactly what all those men were imagining and he hated it.

Now that he'd taken her, her striptease mocked his hold on her, made his own desire seem nothing more or better than what all the other men around him felt. But that couldn't be right, because he liked her, wanted to look out for her. That must count for something. Not that his cock cared about subtleties of feeling. It wanted only one thing and he agreed with it.

Emily had tossed her top to the side, baring all that creamy skin, those sweet little breasts. The song changed to the Stones "Little T & A' and her dancing took on a bawdier feel. Now she looked straight at the audience, a teasing smile on her lips as she danced and shook her tits and ass for them.

Slowly she eased her skirt over her hips and down those glorious legs.

To think he'd been inside all that hot, erotic energy. He'd die if he didn't have her again. Tonight.

He had to grit his teeth as her set ended and men shoved money into her thong and garters, taking the opportunity to run their grubby hands over her. He tried telling himself it was her job, he'd been watching the same thing for eight months now and this was no different, but it didn't ease the urge to kick the shit out of every guy in the place.

He was turning into a fucking cave man. He'd better learn to deal with it, or at least keep his reaction to himself. The crowd responded to her and she was probably making great money. He was glad for her, even though his stomach sank at the thought that the more money she made, the sooner she'd leave.

All the more reason not to waste the time he had.

She left the stage to enthusiastic applause and shouts, appearing five minutes later on the floor. He watched her from the corner of his eye as he worked his way around the room. Her skin shimmered in the light, and she was lightly flushed from her exertions. Just looking at her made him dizzy. When she flirted with customers he had to turn away.

She glanced up every now and then, her eyes searching him out to smile at him. A smile that both calmed him and sent his blood pumping with the thought of having her again. At two o'clock she left the floor and he followed, clocking out before heading back out to the floor where he chatted with Richie. He had the same hours as Emily the nights they worked together, but she needed a few minutes to change, and sometimes she showered.

Fifteen minutes later she appeared in a sleeveless white blouse and red skirt that seemed both innocent and intensely sexy at the same time. Kind of like Emily herself.

She looked around the room, her expression pensive, as if she thought he'd left without her. As if that were possible. A moment later she saw him by the door and she smiled. A full, delighted smile that took his breath away.

She made her way over to him and smiled again, only this time some shyness had crept in.

"I'll walk you home," he said as she neared, conscious of Richie watching them.

Of course, Richie was no fool, but there was no reason to be indiscreet.

"That would be great," she said, her cheeks pinkening before she looked away.

They both said goodnight to Richie and headed out, walking along in silence. Then he took her hand in his. He hadn't planned it, it just seemed like the natural thing to do, and he needed to touch her, to connect with her after watching her from afar.

Emily glanced up at him, her freshly scrubbed face so lovely it hurt to look at her. Still neither of them said anything as they entered the hotel, and the pleasurable tension grew until his skin was humming and every nerve ending was aware of her beside him.

They got on the elevator alone and as soon as the doors closed he pulled her to him. His lips found hers already parted, ready for him, and her hands slid around his neck, holding him close. Her sweet body pressed against his and she tasted so good he got lost in her.

Then the elevator doors opened onto the seventeenth floor and an elderly man got on. They all stood and watched their progress as the numbers above the door changed.

By the time they reached Emily's floor Cutter had forced himself to relax. One of them had to, and it didn't look like it was going to be her. Something had changed and now she seemed anxious, glancing up at him out of the corner of her eye and smiling nervously.

He wasn't sure what that was all about. Was she afraid he was going to open the door and take her against the wall or throw her over a table? As appealing as that was, he wasn't going to lose control this time. He was going to take it slow and make it last, give back a little of the sensual torture she'd shown him.

***

Emily led the way down the hall to her room, her whole body vibrating with awareness. If she'd had any doubts about whether he'd be coming in, that kiss in the elevator had put them to rest. He was as ready as she was, though he didn't seem afflicted by nerves like she was. She wanted him, God she wanted him, but the crazy adrenaline she'd been riding on earlier in the night had given way and now she was just herself, no tricks or costumes, no stripper persona.

He was right behind her as she opened the door and set her things on the table just inside. Now what? Should she saunter over to the bed like some kind of sex goddess, or take off her clothes here? Or maybe she should offer him a drink? Contrary to what she might have led him to believe, she was no good at this sort of thing. What if he ended up disappointed that she wasn't more exciting?

She hadn't even looked at him since they entered her room, but she could feel him right behind her, big and sexy and probably used to crazy hot sex whenever he wanted.

Fortunately, he stopped all thought when he turned her around by the shoulders and kissed her. His lips landed warm and soft on hers, grazing over hers as he let out a hum of pleasure. It was a kiss that demanded nothing, and instantly all her fears fled. Her eyes closed and she leaned into him, her arms wrapping around his chest. One big hand cupped the back of her head as the other pressed the middle of her back, holding her close while his lips continued their unhurried assault.

A little whimper rose from the back of her throat, and her tongue slipped out to trace the seam of his mouth. Immediately he deepened the kiss, his mouth opening over hers as his tongue sought hers. He was greedy but patient, his clever tongue diving deep and then retreating until she was clutching him tighter, moaning for more.

They kissed and kissed, standing in the middle of her room, his body pressed to her along her entire length. He gave just enough, making her crave more before he gave it.

The memory of him stroking inside her made her restless. For the second time that night she went to work on the buttons of his shirt. This time he let her do it herself, though he kissed her senseless all the while, distracting her until she almost forgot her purpose.

Breathless, she pushed his shirt off him and ran her hands down his chest.

"Ever thought of stripping, Cutter? The ladies would pay plenty to see you."

She was only half-kidding. As much as she loved having him to herself, she almost felt bad that his beauty was hidden. Works of art were meant to be seen.

He let out an amused laugh. "I think I'll leave that to you. No one would pay to see me dance."

"I could teach you," she said, teasing him now.

"Okay, then," he said, his expression wicked. "Show me how you take off a shirt."

She looked at him in surprise and then laughed. So he wanted to play, did he? She could do that. Slowly she began unbuttoning her blouse, all the while singing the bawdy tune everyone thought of when it came to stripping. Da da da dada...She flipped her hair and spun, snaking her hips down to the floor and then coming up to smile wickedly at him. Her watched her as he always did, only instead of the reluctant watchfulness she usually saw, there was only heat.

She played him a little longer, holding the blouse closed even after the buttons were all released, then showing just a shoulder. He took a step toward her and reached for her hip but she darted away, still singing as she flung the shirt across the bed. His eyes went wide when he saw she was braless. She was laughing as he came after her wearing a wolfish grin, clearly determined to catch her. She didn't try very hard to get away and in seconds he had her cornered by the kitchenette.

She yelped as he scooped her up and dropped her on the bed. She bounced once and then he was on top of her, his big hands gripping her wrists and holding her down. Instinctively she arched against him, unable to get enough contact. She wanted to own every inch of that smooth skin, that hard, rangy muscle.

But he had other plans. Holding her wrists trapped he bent down and captured her breast in his mouth, letting out a groan of pleasure as he sucked and nipped at her. The sight of him feasting on her was so erotic she whimpered again and tried to free herself.

"Please, I need to touch you."

He looked down at her, his eyes dark and full of a heat that sent another rush of awareness along her sensitized skin. "Now you know how I felt during your lap dance. Do you have any idea what you did to me?"

She writhed under him, smiling at his quick intake of breath. "I know exactly what I did. You can thank me later."

He growled and moved to her other breast, clearly planning more delicious torment. Only he was having trouble controlling himself. She could feel it in the tension that radiated from him, hear it in his ragged breathing. And then there was his cock. Good God, he was so hard and heavy where he pressed into her, she nearly screamed with impatience.

Finally he released her hands and moved lower, kissing his way down her body until he got to her skirt. Unsnapping it he pulled it over her hips and down her legs, gazing at every inch of her skin like he was going to eat her right up. She spread her legs wider and lifted her hips, bringing his gaze back to the black bikini underwear she wore, the last barrier between them.

"I'm going to drive you crazy and then I'm going to bury myself so deep in you, I may never come out."

Emily shot upwards, frantic now to be closer to him, but he only laughed, as if bemused by what they did to each other.

"Not just yet, baby. I've been wanting to do this since the first time I saw you."

Backing down the bed he grabbed hold of one of her feet. His gaze seared into hers as he stroked his calloused hands from ankle to calf, his lips following in a lazy trail. Gently he bit and licked his way up, lifting her leg until it rested over his shoulder before making his way up her thigh.

Her skin burned everywhere he touched, and she was panting, her body restless with need. Then his dark head settled between her legs and he spread her open, licking into her. He'd barely touched her and she was sobbing with need, saying his name over and over as her fingers wove into his silky hair.

"You taste so good," he murmured, sounding his approval when she lifted her hips into him.

He was slow, taking his time even when she didn't want him too, keeping just behind her rhythm until she thought she might die. His tongue dove into her slick channel again and again as if he were drinking her up, then came back to lick and suck on her throbbing clit.

Her body was strung tight, her fingers rigid in his hair when he slid one finger, then a second into her and thrust in time with his tongue. She broke over the peak with waves of pleasure that pulsed from his fingers and tongue, wracking her body in a long and nearly painful release that left her limp and dazed beneath him.

Chapter Six

When she finally opened her eyes Cutter was naked and poised above her, his dark eyes intent on her. His cock was huge and hard and already sheathed in a condom. She couldn't wait for him to be inside her.

If only she had the energy to move.

"Do anything you want to me," she said, waving her hand weakly. "You've earned it."

He laughed in surprise and smiled wickedly down at her. "Oh, I will, trust me."

Leaning his weight onto his forearms he kissed her, a deep, lush kiss that stirred her up again. Her hands rose to glide down his back as she opened for him, the tide of her desire rising luxuriously.

He entered her in one sure thrust, a deep, satisfied groan escaping him. And even though he'd earned a quick finish, he waited for her, stroking her slow and steady and deep until she was right there with him. Her legs lifted straight into the air and her hands clamped around his ass, urging him deeper and harder. He hooked one arm around her thigh and pressed her leg up until it was on her chest, driving himself into her with abandon.

Once again her orgasm crashed over her. She held him deep inside her as she pulsed around him, his big gorgeous body trembling with need and control. Then her muscles relaxed and he rose up on his hands and thrust into her twice more, his body shuddering over hers before collapsing.

They lay there like that for several minutes, Emily with her arms around Cutter as their breathing slowed to normal. Then her stomach growled. She nipped his shoulder, rousing him from his stupor.

"Hey, want to order room service? I'm starving."

Cutter rolled off her and looked at her through heavy-lidded eyes. She sat up to get a better look at him. Jesus, he was sexy. Definitely the sexiest guy she'd ever laid her hands on. Would he want to stay the night, what was left of it anyway? Or was this strictly sex?

Cutter smiled lazily up at her. "Room service sounds awesome." He looked her over as she knelt beside him and his eyes got that look again. "Damn, girl, you are unbelievable. You'd better put something on or I swear to God I'm going to ravish you again. I already have several different ways I want to take you."

She stayed right where she was for several long moments, caught by his gaze. But then she roused herself. As tempting as it would be to let him do what he'd threatened, she really was hungry, and she wasn't sure she could go another round with Cutter without some sustenance. He was definitely a workout.

Emily called down and ordered a BLT for herself, a decadent choice by her standards. Cutter requested a burger and fries, to regain his manly vigor he told her, waggling his eyebrows as he fell back against the pillow.

It was a silly side of him she'd never have guessed at, and one that made him all the more appealing. Their food wouldn't be up for at least half an hour, so Emily filled the Jacuzzi tub and they lolled in the hot water and bubbles, each of them at an end so they could face one another. They talked a bit but mostly they sat there, dazed and sated and smiling.

When room service knocked on the door forty-five minutes later, Cutter jumped out of the water before Emily could rouse herself. Wrapping himself in a white robe from the back of the door, he took the tray from the employee and dug cash out of his wallet to pay for it.

Emily sat on the bed next to Cutter, the two of them propped up on pillows as they ate. It was nearly five a.m. when she licked the last bit of mayonnaise off her fingers. She looked over at Cutter and laughed.

"Do I look as exhausted as you do?" she asked, taking in the dark circles under his eyes.

He yawned and looked at her. "No, you look sleepy and gorgeous. You're not human."

Emily raised an eyebrow. "Hmm. I'll take that as a compliment. But I still need to go to bed. Care to make this a sleepover?" she asked.

Cutter's smile was wide and pleased.

"Hell, yes I'll sleep over. Thank God I don't have a job tomorrow. What do you say we don't even set the alarm?"

"Deal," she said, her blood singing at how easy it was to be with him. "You're kind of on my side though. Can we switch?"

"Whatever you say, hot stuff," he said. Getting up off the bed he discarded his robe and came around to the other side. "My only rule is that we're both naked."

Good lord, the man was glorious. His dark hair was mussed, his eyes sleepy and utterly sexy, his skin glowing in the light from the bedside lamp. How was she going to sleep beside such a specimen?

It had been nearly a year since she'd slept, literally or biblically, with a man. She was out of practice and worried she'd do something wrong. What if she'd developed a snore, or ground her teeth like she had as a kid?

She scooted across to the other side of the bed, still naked but under the covers, and watched as he closed the drapes, blocking out all the light from the Strip, and climbed in beside her. Neither one of them made any noise about brushing their teeth. Emily was tired beyond caring, and somehow it seemed too civilized, too clean for the kind of night they'd had. Rolling over she turned out the light. A strong arm snaked over her waist and pulled her to him so that she lay on his arm, her head on his chest.

"Goodnight, Emily," he murmured, his breath sighing across her hair.

"Goodnight, Cutter," she whispered, her eyes fluttering closed.

Emily came awake sometime later with a bladder ready to burst and a desperate need for water. The room was still dark in the way hotel rooms were when you pulled the heavy curtains. It could have been anytime of day or night, and Emily considered trying to go back to sleep without peeing. Then she looked at the clock and saw it was almost noon.

Cutter was still asleep, his face buried in the pillow, the sheets down around his waist. As tempting as it was to wake him, he probably needed the sleep. He'd said something about having put a roof on someone's house yesterday morning, which meant he'd had an even longer day than she had.

Moving as quietly as possible she went to the bathroom and cleaned up. Her hair was a rat's nest, but she kind of liked it. It made her look so much wilder than she really was, a wildcat who could lure in a man like Cutter. Then again, she really had done that, so maybe she was wilder than she'd always thought.

She got the coffee going and threw a camisole and shorts on, then started in on her barre work. She was sore this morning, sore in places she hadn't been for a while. She started off small, letting her body warm up and lengthen.

Sheets rustled behind her and she turned around to see Cutter watching her, his head propped on one arm.

"Good morning," he smiled, his voice deep with sleep. "You look amazing. Are you always this frisky in the morning?"

"We slept through the morning, but yes, I am. And I'm feeling friskier by the minute," she said, climbing into the bed with him.

His eyes widened in surprise and then a delighted grin spread across his face. She pushed him down on his back and straddled him.

"You ever do those exercises naked?" he asked, his hands skimming down her sides to rest on her hips.

"You see me naked for hours every week. Isn't that enough?"

"Hell, no. There is no enough," he said, his hips thrusting up into her.

She could feel him hard and ready beneath the blanket draped across his hips. Putting her hands on his chest she slid up the length of him, letting him press into her. Over and over she did it until they were both breathing hard. His hands gripped her hips, holding her to him and he bent his knees for more leverage.

"Take everything off right now," he demanded, his restless hands sliding over her breasts.

Standing up so that she was looking straight down at him and giving him an excellent view, she pulled off her camisole and shorts. Cutter pushed the blanket off and sat up, pulling her to him until his face was buried in her thatch of dark blond hair. Her hands gripped his shoulders as he parted her with his thumbs and licked her slow and deep.

Emily lasted only a minute before her knees gave out and she fell into his lap. Then she remembered.

"Oh, God. I don't have any condoms. I didn't think anything would happen and then..."

"Not to worry. I swiped a handful from that box in the storage closet. I tossed a few on the nightstand there."

"My hero," she said, grabbing a packet and ripping it open.

Slowly, tormenting him just a bit, she rolled the condom on and then rose up above him, lowering onto him slowly, absorbing the feel of him as he filled her. As small as she was compared to him, on top of him she felt powerful, every move she made causing the most delicious reaction in him.

Pulling her over him, he took a breast into his mouth, sucking and teasing it with his tongue even as his hand found the wet heat between her legs. Within seconds she was ready to come, every sound they made, every place his skin came in contact with hers – the inside of her thighs, the brush of his fingers, his mouth on her breasts – added up to an exquisite sensory overload that built until it she couldn't contain it any longer.

She cried out, her back arching as her hands reached back to balance her weight on his thighs. When she opened her eyes Cutter was looking at her with predatory intensity. Holding her hips, he thrust several more times and then moaned his own release.

***

Sometime after eating lunch, screwing again and falling asleep for close to an hour, Cutter finally got up. Picking his clothes off the floor he dressed, his eyes never leaving Emily. She'd put on one of the hotel robes, the same one he'd worn last night, and it billowed around her delicate frame. Her hair fell loose around her shoulders and her eyes were a clear, startling blue. No one looking at her now would believe what a tiger should could be. Or was it a lion?

"So how long exactly are you planning to be here?" he asked, the question out of his mouth before his brain had time to vet it.

She looked startled, the little smile she'd had fading away.

"Probably three weeks or so," she said, looking uncomfortable. "I figure I'll have enough money by then to breathe a bit easier. I can't stay much longer than that since I have an apartment waiting for me."

"I guess we'd better make the most of the next few weeks, then," he said. "Want to hang after work tonight?"

"You bet. It's going to be hard enough keeping my hands off you for hours. I need something to look forward to."

"I'll see you at six, then."

Emily came toward him, wrapping her arms around his neck. He pulled her in close for a long, slow kiss, already missing her.

When they finally came up for air she stepped back, flushed and breathless, and it was all he could do to make himself leave.

Back home he showered and changed, then took care of things around the house, all the while replaying last night's delights. It had been incredible, so great he couldn't help dwelling on the fact that his time with her was limited.

But that was fine. They'd have a good time while it lasted. Women like her didn't come along every day. He was lucky to know her at all, and he would just enjoy whatever time he had with her. This was, after all, pretty much the male fantasy, a no-strings-attached fling with a gorgeous, sexy woman. He wasn't going to turn into a sappy jackass about it.

He went back to her hotel room after work that night and the next and each time was just as hot and heavy as the first. Unfortunately, he had a couple of jobs lined up Tuesday and Wednesday, which meant he was a zombie at the worksite from lack of sleep. It was a wonder he didn't saw off his own hand.

He didn't work at the club on Wednesdays, though, and neither one of them broached the idea of getting together before Sunday night. He thought about asking her to get together sometime before they worked together again on Sunday, but second-guessed himself. Maybe it was better to keep it a strictly sex after work scenario.

Friday night he shot some pool with Frank and Scott at their favorite dive bar, but he played lousy, too distracted by thoughts of Emily. He caught shit about it, too, since the two of them had been waiting for him the night he jumped Emily's bones in the closet. He'd gone back out to the floor thinking he looked presentable, but it hadn't fooled them.

"Dude, did you just get laid?" Scott had asked, as impressed as he ever got.

"In my dreams," Cutter replied, never one to kiss and tell.

But it didn't matter what he said. They knew, and they felt free to give him all kinds of shit.

"Are you thinking about that chick?" Frank asked after he missed an easy bank shot. "Not that I'd blame you, but try to focus, would you? It's no fun whipping your ass when you're not trying."

Cutter usually beat them both, it was just a matter of by how much, but tonight his vivid memory was too distracting. He lost every game and had to put up with much head-shaking from his friends. He considered calling Emily on his way home but decided eleven o'clock was too late for it to be anything but a booty call, which seemed kind of lame.

By Saturday morning he was in a state of withdrawal. He needed to see Emily and he didn't much care how or where. He made himself wait until after ten and then he called her. A current of heat shot through him at the sound of her voice.

"If you're not doing anything tonight, I was thinking I could make you dinner," he said, trying to sound casual, like it was no big deal.

"Like a real, home-cooked meal, in a home?" she asked, the pleasure in her voice making him smile.

"That's right. From scratch and everything."

"I wouldn't miss it."

"Excellent. Any requests, allergies, hidden traumas related to food?"

Emily laughed, the sound husky and low. His cock throbbed in response.

"I'm not feeling real picky. A grilled cheese sandwich would make my day at this point."

"Now that's what I like to hear. Are you okay getting here? If not I can come get you."

"I'll be fine. It'll be good to get my car out on the road."

Cutter gave her his address and directions and told her to come by at seven. As soon as he hung up he started planning. He was no gourmet, but he had a few things up his sleeve and he could follow a recipe as well as anyone.

***

Emily hung up her phone and danced around the room. She'd spent the last three days determined to give Cutter space and not seem needy. He had a life here after all, and the last thing she wanted was to seem like a lonely looser. Also, let's face it, she needed the rest after the stretch of scorching nights they'd had together. But three nights apart was more than enough, especially when she had nothing to take her mind off how good it was with him.

And it was good, better than good. It made her question her plans, reevaluate how long she should stick around. Between Cutter and the money she was bringing in, she had powerful motivators for not leaving town. Which in effect meant not getting on with her life.

But she didn't want to think about that. She had a date with Cutter. Not only that, she would finally have a real meal, and one with another human being, no less. It was enough to make her giddy as she worked on her routines for the coming week.

Then it was time to get ready for dinner. Her dinner date. When was the last time she'd been on a date? Of course, they'd done the crazy sex part before the first date, but whatever.

She threw open her closet and rifled through every article of clothing she had, looking for something casual yet classy. Something unstripper-like. Finally she settled on a sky blue halter-top sundress that ended at her knees and a pair of blue sandals with little pink flowers that matched her toenail polish. She twisted her hair into a loose chignon and added a pair of dangly silver earrings with little bluebirds on the ends. A touch of lip gloss, blush and a swipe of mascara and she was ready to go.

She waited for the elevator, so excited she all but tap-danced. The last time she'd felt this way was a year ago when she was dancing a new ballet, one that had been created especially for her. The possibilities had been endless, all of it completely new and never before seen. And like any live performance, you never knew exactly what would happen next.

The valet brought her car around and then she was off, stopping for a couple of bottles of wine before heading northwest into the part of the city regular people lived. She'd barely been outside of the Strip the entire time she'd been in Vegas, and even then she hadn't gone far, just to the mechanic, a supermarket and a costume shop for Vegas performers. She'd assumed, quite wrongly she now realized, that the whole city looked more or less the same.

At first she found the landscape dull and ugly, but as she drove she began to appreciate the sparse beauty of the unfamiliar plant life. After her weeks on the Strip, it was a relief to see regular houses in neighborhoods where children rode their bikes and dogs raced after them.

Cutter lived about twenty minutes from her hotel. She turned onto his street, surprised to find he lived in a quiet residential neighborhood, one where the houses looked fairly prosperous and had generous amounts of land surrounding them and ensuring privacy.

She parked her car in front of his house, a hacienda style a little bigger than your average ranch house. Rock gardens took up most of the front yard, with tall grasses filling the places in between. A paved walkway led from the driveway to the front entrance.

Cutter opened the door before she even had a chance to knock. He smiled at her, beamed really, and instantly her nervousness evaporated, replaced by pure joy. In deference to the heat he wore olive green cargo shorts and a red t-shirt. How in the world was she going to make it through dinner like a civilized person without jumping his bones?

He stepped aside to let her in, taking the wine from her before pulling her to him for a deep, knee-weakening kiss that left her breathless.

"You look amazing. If it wasn't for the fact that I have food cooking, I would drag your gorgeous bod straight to my bed," he said, looking at her like he might devour her anyway.

She stepped away from him. "We can do this. We're adults, right? Besides, I'm starving and whatever it is you're cooking smells amazing."

Cutter acceded to her wishes, though his gaze raked her approvingly, looking at her as if drinking her in. When they finally made it to the bed, it would definitely be worth the wait. But she'd been looking forward to having something resembling a normal date. As much fun as it was to eye each other all night at the club and then tear each other's clothes off back in her room, she was looking forward to talking.

"I'll give you the grand tour first," he said, leading her down a short hallway into the kitchen.

It was spacious and sunny with tiled floors, high ceilings, and a large island in the middle. It opened into a dining area and generous living room. Southwestern style rugs in earth tones covered the floors and red-hued clay vases and jugs sat on tables here and there. Most striking were a series of framed black and white photographs of kids playing kickball, men and women smoking cigarettes outside a run-down house as the sun set behind them.

"I took those," he said, nodding toward the photos.

"They're beautiful. Is that where you lived with your mother?"

"Most of them were taken on the reservation near Carson City, where I grew up. A couple were taken on a Washoe rez in California where a few cousins live. I was really into photography for a while in my twenties, but I haven't done much in the last few years."

He had a good eye and the photos seemed to be looking its the subjects with affection, but there was no mistaking the underlying poverty in the surroundings. It was her first bit of insight into where he came from, but now wasn't the time to grill him on his childhood.

"This place is gorgeous, Cutter. You've really done something amazing here."

"I spent about a year's worth of weekends building it, but it was worth it."

"You built this yourself?" she asked, floored by the idea. Imagine creating something as concrete as a house. Dance was so ephemeral, with nothing but the memory to show for it in the end.

"It was kind of a dream I had for a while. I figured if I was building houses for complete strangers, I ought to do it for myself."

"It's bigger than I was expecting for a bachelor's lair," she said, peering into one of three bedrooms at the back of the house. Like many houses in the area, this one spread out on one floor in deference to the heat.

He shrugged a shoulder. "I decided if I was going to do it, I'd make sure it was one I'd want to live in for the duration. Who knows? There may be more than just me one day," he said.

He looked away, as if he'd revealed too much.

"You did a beautiful job," she replied softly, touched at the thought of him creating a home for some future family.

A hollow seemed to open in her chest that it wouldn't be her, couldn't be her. She'd be long gone, barely a memory by then. She gazed into the last bedroom, sparsely furnished with a twin bed and chest of drawers. But instead she saw what it could be, a child's room with walls covered in bright pictures, a bookshelf with stories to be read before bed.

They were quiet as they returned to the kitchen.

"I hope you like lasagna," he said, opening the oven to peek inside.

Heavenly smells wafted out. Emily let out a deep sigh of appreciation.

"Who doesn't love lasagna? I just haven't eaten it since I was about eleven. When I was dancing I was always watching my weight. I feel like I've been pigging out for months now, but it's so nice to be able to eat good food."

Cutter quirked an eyebrow at her as he looked her up and down.

"If this is how you look when you pig out, then I'm happy to help feed you."

"Good. Maybe you'll invite me back again."

"Oh, you can count on that," he said, his heated look stopping her breath.

The chemistry between them was as potent now as before they'd started their fling. It seemed counter-intuitive, like they should have diffused all the sexual tension by now, but nothing of the sort had happened. Now the tension contained the knowledge of what was possible between them, memories of how crazy they made one another.

Overwhelmed by the constant hunger, the utter craving he called forth from her, she turned away. It didn't matter how vital he made her feel, it couldn't last, no more than a dance could last after the lights went up.

From behind her she heard Cutter leave the room, then the soft croon of a saxophone. Coltrane, if she wasn't mistaken. The music's sensual throb surrounded her, loosening her limbs. She would take things one day at a time and enjoy pleasure where she found it. What was the point of anticipating pain while they were still together?

Chapter Seven

"Everything all right?" Cutter asked, coming in from the other room.

"Absolutely."

"Then let's eat."

They sat together at a round wooden table in front of glass doors that led to a generous deck and the backyard beyond. The lasagna was delicious, so homey and substantial she felt the burn of tears behind her eyes and had to distract herself with conversation.

"So is it just you and your sister here, or do you have other family in the area?"

As soon as she asked, it struck her how odd it was that they'd never exchanged even this basic information. She knew so little about him.

"Just me and my sister. My mom's still on the rez and my dad's in Reno. I came here right after college. There was so much building going on then it was easy to find work. Lisa ran into some trouble in Carson City and came here."

Emily looked at him questioningly, not sure if she should ask what sort of trouble he was talking about. Cutter hesitated but then continued, his face schooled to show no emotion.

"When I was fifteen I went to live with my dad in Reno but Lisa stayed with my mom. Things were fine for a few years but by the time Lisa turned sixteen I think she was already in pretty bad shape. I was in college by then and my mom was too out of it to notice or do anything about it. I didn't even know Lisa had started into heavy drugs until a friend of mine ran into her. She was strung out on heroine and stripping in a place that makes the Pink Pussycat look like a palace."

His face contorted with emotion and he stopped talking as if unable to go on. He scrubbed his face with his hands as if he could wipe away all feeling.

"Never mind," she said, putting her hand on his. "You don't have to tell me everything."

But he seemed to want to get it all out now.

"It was another year before she let me help her, and probably another year before she was clean. She lived with me for a while but she's doing great now and has her own place. She waits tables and goes to school part-time."

He stopped and shot her a wry look. "I don't usually have to pick her up at work but her car was in the shop."

"I wasn't even going to mention it," Emily said, smiling as she speared a piece of salad with her fork. "I'm glad she's doing so well. She's lucky to have you."

"If I hadn't left I could have protected her better."

"Maybe, but maybe not. There's a good chance it wouldn't have mattered. Plus, you made something of yourself and were in a better position to help her."

He looked surprised. "I never thought of it that way." He paused, considering. "Maybe you're right. I think I'd have gotten into some bad shit myself if I'd stayed. My dad seemed to think so anyway."

"Was it so bad growing up on the reservation?"

"It's complicated, and it's taken me a long time to sort it out. I think that's why I took those pictures. Looking back I can see how little people talked about the future, how hopeless we all felt. Everyone was poor so as a kid I didn't think too much about that part, not until I went to a new high school. It got harder to go back after that. Plus my mother fits right into the stereotype of the alcoholic Indian, so there's that. But there's not a day that goes by I don't feel guilty about leaving, even if it was the best thing for me."

"Do you ever visit?" she asked.

"I visit my mom every couple of months. It's always rough, though. She's not an easy woman and time hasn't been good to her. Or rather, she hadn't been good to herself."

"So is your sister the reason you took the job at the club?" she asked.

"You mean am I working there to make up for the fact that I couldn't protect Lisa?"

"Sorry. I don't mean to sound like an armchair psychologist.

"That's okay. I can see how it might look like I was trying to atone for past mistakes or something, but it's nothing like that. I was putting an addition on Steve's house and we got to talking. This was when things had started to go downhill with the housing market, and I mentioned how few houses were being built. He offered me the job and I took it. It was more in spite of what had happened to Lisa than because of it."

Cutter stopped and looked at her plate. "Have you had enough?"

"God, yes. That was delicious, but I've hit the wall."

Cutter beamed at her. "You liked it?"

"That was the best thing I've had in years. Where'd you learn to cook?" she asked.

"I hate to admit it, but this is pretty much the only thing I can cook. I ate lasagna once at a friend's house and it rocked my world. I learned how to make it so I could have it whenever I wanted."

"Are you saying this is the beginning and end of your repertoire?"

"Well, I can also roast a chicken and cook a steak. And I can grill."

"You are such a guy. But that's fine, since it's not your cooking I'm after," she said, batting her eyes at him.

Cutter laughed and stood up to clear the table. Emily followed suit, carrying dishes to the sink.

"Driving out here was the first time since I got here that I didn't think all of Las Vegas was awful," Emily said, covering the salad in plastic wrap as she spoke. "Maybe it's because it's so different from what I'm used to, but I just can't imagine living here."

She glanced up from to see Cutter looking at her in surprise as water ran from the sink faucet.

"Oh God, I'm sorry. I didn't mean to send so judgmental. Obviously plenty of people like it out here..." She trailed off, feeling as if she'd written herself into a corner.

Cutter leaned back against the counter, looking thoughtful. "I'm not surprised you feel that way. I mean, you've been living in a hotel on the Strip and working at the Pink Pussycat. But that's not how people actually live around here. There are neighborhoods and parks and sights people come from all over to see. Plus there's more culture here than you probably realize. Did you know we have two ballet companies here?"

Cutter stopped, his expression sheepish.

"Actually I do know. My mother thinks I'm working at one of them. But you're right," Emily said, feeling foolish. "It's arrogant to think I know a place when I haven't taken the trouble to see anything."

"Maybe we can see some of the sights while you're here. It's too hot now for most of the outdoor stuff, but in the next couple of weeks or so it'll start to cool down. Maybe we could even go camping in Red Rock Canyon."

"Camping? As in sleeping in tents?"

Cutter laughed. "As in sleeping in tents. But you don't sound too psyched."

"I've just never done it is all. I can't decide if it would be fun or miserable."

"Maybe a little of both," he said, coming toward her. He put his hands on her hips and whispered in her ear, his voice low and husky, as if he were trying to seduce her. "I'll set up the tent, stomping around and swearing because I'm missing a crucial part. We'll eat a dinner of canned hash and then crawl into the tent and snuggle together inside, where it'll be roughly a hundred and twenty degrees. You'll sleep fitfully and hate me by morning. What do you say?"

"You are seriously turning me on," she said, throwing her arms around his neck.

She meant it as a joke, but actually, she *was* turned on. She'd been turned on since she walked through the door. Since she met him.

Cutter pressed her back against the island until she felt him fully against her. He was already hard, his breath quickening as those deft hands of his skimmed beneath her skirt to the back of her thighs. Everywhere he touched heated until she was burning for him.

Her hands dug into his hair and she urged him closer, her tongue sliding into his mouth to taste his heat and spice.

Without warning he lifted her onto the counter and stepped between her spread thighs, his restless hands pushing her skirt up around her waist until she was bared to him, nothing between them but the scrap of her pink lace underwear. Panting now, her hands worked at the snap of his shorts until she held his huge cock in her hand. With her other hand she pulled him toward her.

"Please. I need you now," she whimpered.

"Hang on. I need to get a condom. I can't –"

"It's okay. We don't need one anymore," she said, wrapping her legs around his hips.

He looked at her blankly, as if I afraid to believe what he was hearing. She was so crazed with lust it took great effort to focus and explain.

"Remember that talk we had about how we're both healthy? I made an appointment at the health clinic the day after and now I have an IUD."

Cutter's eyes narrowed, sharpening with fierce intent as he yanked her underwear aside and slid into her with one firm stroke, the friction of his shorts rubbing against her inner thighs only adding to her sensory overload.

"Christ you feel good," he groaned, red flags of color high on his cheeks. "So hot and wet for me."

Falling back onto the counter, she took him as far into her as he could go, her knees drawn up to feel every inch of him. This wasn't gentle or controlled, not romantic or practiced. It was three days of need built up until neither of them knew anything but the striving together of their bodies.

Cutter leaned over her and took her nipple in his mouth, rolling it as he stroked into her again and again, his thumb sliding over her clit so that every part of her was taken over by him.

"That's it, baby, come for me," he urged, and the sound of his voice, his warm breath on her skin, sent her over.

Her body arched off the counter, pulsing on and on as she sobbed with release. She held him through his peak, his whole body shuddering over her as he gave an ecstatic groan and collapsed onto her, his head resting on her breast.

They lay there like that, sweaty and sated, and it was several minutes before either of them spoke. Finally Cutter raised his head and looked at her.

"The dishes can wait. You're going to get into my bed and we're going to screw until neither of us can see straight."

"Whatever you say."

***

By the time Cutter got out of the shower the next morning, Emily was standing in the kitchen in his old Lallapalooza t-shirt, her brow furrowed in concentration as she sliced onions. A carton of eggs sat on the counter and the toaster ticked and emitted a cheery red glow.

Her head bobbed lightly to the Stones' "Let it Bleed" and he watched, mesmerized, as her hips moved and she instinctively, thoughtlessly, swung her hips around in a manner more subtle but no less erotic than her stage show. Jesus, the woman could move.

She didn't even realize he was there until he wrapped his arms around her from behind. She started in surprise and then laughed lightly, relaxing instantly into his arms. "You Got the Silver" started to play, Keith Richards singing, and Cutter held Emily close and swayed with her.

Turning around she smiled up at him, wrapping her arms around his waist as she leaned her cheek on his chest. It was the first time he'd danced with her, but it felt perfect, natural, like making love.

She yelped in shock when he grabbed her waist and swung her around, her head falling back as she squealed in delight. When he finally put her back on her feet they kept moving, and all at once he understood why the human race danced.

Sometimes you just had to move, there were no words for what you felt.

They spun around the kitchen floor, a current flowing between them until he felt her heartbeat in his, the thrum of her blood as if it flowed though his own veins. They were laughing and breathless when the song ended, clinging to each other for several more moments.

They both sniffed the air at the same time, frowning.

"Something's burning!" Emily squealed, pulling away to turn to the stove.

Fortunately, it was just the toast, and soon they were sitting down to breakfast. They chatted about the club, making fun of Steve as usual, but mostly Cutter just tried not to stare at her like a crushed-out kid. He didn't want her to leave and was afraid that any minute she'd announce it was time to go.

"What do you think about staying here?" he asked, finally voicing an idea he'd been turning over in his head for the last week.

Emily looked up from her paper, the piece of toast she'd been about to bite into arrested in mid-air.

"You mean move in with you?"

His heart rate, already faster than usual from nerves, kicked into high gear.

"You said yourself you're sick to death of living in a hotel. Besides, this wouldn't cost you anything. There's more than enough room here for two people, and you could take one of the extra rooms if you like so you'd have your own space."

He watched as surprise and uncertainty passed over her face. He held his breath, his mind racing with other benefits to convince her. But he didn't want to push her too hard. She either liked the idea or she didn't.

Maybe he was hoping that it would be so great while she was living with him, she'd change her mind about leaving. But that motivation was so pathetic he pushed it down and hoped it never saw the light of day again. He didn't have anything to offer her. He worked too much for too little money, and was just barely keeping himself above water when it came to the house. Besides, she came from a whole other world, one she'd be returning to soon. They were better off a temporary thing.

She was biting her lip. "I am sick of the Strip. Lately I've been feeling like I'd jump out the hotel window if it weren't hermetically sealed."

Cautious hope rose in his chest, but he didn't want to let it loose until she fully agreed. It would be better, in fact, if he didn't set it loose at all. This was going to be the most casual of arrangements. Nothing to get all worked up about. Maybe something had happened out in the garden last night, but that didn't mean there'd be a happily ever after. What it guaranteed, in fact, was more pain all around. But it was worth it.

Emily folded and refolded her napkin as she worked it all out. Cutter got up and poured himself another cup of coffee and tried to act like he wasn't anxious as hell for her decision.

He moved around the kitchen, feigning nonchalance, but finally Emily looked up at him with a shy smile. "Okay. If you really want me here, I'd love to stay."

He couldn't help the smile that spread across his face. He only hoped it didn't reveal too much.

***

Emily stood on Cutter's doorstep the next morning, a suitcase and two duffel bags at her feet, her stomach fluttering with a combination of nerves and excitement as she knocked.

The door opened a few seconds later and Cutter stood there grinning in a pair of brown cargo shorts and snug-fitting black tee shirt. Emily's mouth went dry.

"Hey, gorgeous. Come on in," he said, grabbing all three bags before standing back for her to enter.

Together they walked down the hall until they stood between the two spare rooms.

"Which room would you like?" he asked.

"I'll take this one," she said, pointing to the room that hadn't made her think about little Cutter offspring.

Cutter set her bags down and looked around, frowning.

"I hope this is okay. If I'd had more time I would have made it a little more comfortable –"

"This is perfect. Besides, unless you turn into the world's loudest snorer, I'm not planning on spending all that much time in here. I'm looking forward to having that gorgeous body of yours to myself every night."

Cutter's eyes glinted wickedly. "Just at night?" he asked, walking toward her until she was backed up against the bed.

Emily was instantly breathless, her limbs softening with surrender. As if in slow motion she fell back onto the neatly made blue bedspread, Cutter following her down. The raw male heat he emanated saturated her senses, leaving her instantly ready. He must have felt the same urgency, for his mouth covered hers in a deep, full-blooded kiss that left her ears ringing and her body taut with need. A work-roughened hand skimmed up her thigh beneath her skirt, settling over her underwear before slipping beneath the thin material.

Deftly he parted her, discovering her readiness with a deep groan into her mouth. Emily's body arched upward and her head fell back, her head spinning with lust. Then his finger began to move and she went from ready to frenzied in a heartbeat.

Her hands moved to the waistband of his shorts, desperate to have him inside her. Cutter drew back, looking at her with dark intensity, his breath hissing out as her hands found him, huge and hard and as ready as she was.

She gasped as he pulled her underwear off and entered her, driving her up the bed. Each stroke brought her closer to the brink without sending her over. Her arms and legs were wrapped around him as she called him name, urging him on.

"I know what you need," he whispered in her ear.

Pulling out of her, he turned her over until she was flat on her belly. Then he slid into her, taking her deep and hard.

"Is that good, baby?" he crooned, but she was beyond words.

His body covered hers so that they were still skin to skin, heat on heat. Then his hand reached around and found her again, slick and wet. She cried out as his fingers slid over her in time with his thrusts and her thoughts narrowed until all she knew were pleasure and need. Higher and higher he took her until her orgasm rushed up to meet her and she cried out with a release that shook through her. Cutter thrust into her to the hilt, his hands clasping hers as he pulsed inside her.

Together they collapsed onto the bed, and it was many minutes before either of them moved. Finally Emily heaved herself up on an elbow to look at Cutter.

"I think this is going to work out just fine," she said.

They didn't have long to indulge themselves, however, as Cutter had a roofing job to finish up before going to the club that night. She was in the middle of unpacking when he came into the room dressed in his jeans, work boots, and a white tee shirt. He pulled her in for a quick kiss.

"I'll be back by four-thirty so we can drive in together. Will you be all right here?"

"Of course. I still have to practice my dances, plus ransack your drawers for old love letters and sexual paraphernalia."

Cutter grinned, momentarily stopping her heart.

"Knock yourself out, babe."

Emily was still smiling when the door closed behind him. He made everything so easy. Unlike with other men she'd dated, she could be herself and let down her guard. Nothing seemed to faze him.

She'd never lived with a man before, not romantically anyway, but the way her past relationships had gone, she'd assumed it would be awkward, with an initial period where they worked out rules and set limits. She soon realized it wouldn't be like that at all with him. Of course, she no longer had a grueling career that made ridiculous demands on her, but it was a pleasant surprise to discover that she wasn't so bad at being with someone, even if he was a temporary someone.

Whereas before she always felt pulled between what her boyfriends wanted and what she wanted, now she found the two things most often being the same. Not that Cutter was her boyfriend, as she sometimes had to remind herself. Still, she wanted to make him happy, and went out of her way to cook meals around his crazy schedule. She wanted to make his days easier when he came home tired from his first job and had to go to the second one. There was no doubt he appreciated all her efforts, but he wasn't taking it for granted.

This became crystal clear when he called her at four o'clock in the afternoon, a week after she'd moved in, to tell her his truck had broken down.

"You head to the club without me. The tow won't be here for another forty-five minutes, and then I'll still need to get a ride home. If I'm lucky I'll only be an hour late to work."

Emily could hear the sounds of traffic on his end.

"Where are you?"

"About a half hour north of Vegas. It looks like it's the radiator, so I'm not going anywhere."

"In other words, you're stranded on the side of the highway, sweating your balls off," Emily said.

Cutter laughed. "That about sums it up."

"Then I'm coming to get you. Tell me where you are."

"You don't need to do that. You'll be late and it's way out of your way."

"Would you let me bake in the desert sun if it was me stuck out there?" she asked, somewhat irritated now. It was actually kind of a bummer that he expected so little of her.

There was a hesitation. "Uh, no. Of course I'd come get you."

"Exactly. So tell me where you are."

By the time she pulled into the breakdown lane behind his truck he looked pretty wilted. Wearily, he climbed into the car and they sat in the cool of her air conditioning, waiting for the tow truck to come.

"You must be exhausted," she said, taking in his dusty work pants and sweat soaked hair. "Maybe someone can fill in for you tonight so you can go home and rest."

"Nah, it's too last-minute. Besides, I could use the money."

This depressed them both and they were silent for a minute.

"Good thing you're not a stark white cracker like me," she said, trying to inject some humor. "I'd have burnt to a crisp out there."

Cutter cackled and pulled her to him, planting a solid kiss on her mouth.

"You're not just any cracker, sweetheart. You're a high-class table wafer, the kind people eat with caviar."

"Oh, speaking of food, I brought dinner. If we eat in the car we won't be quite so late."

She pulled a little cooler from the back seat and set it between them.

"There's pasta salad with artichoke hearts, chipotle chicken wings and brownies. Oh, and a seltzer water for you."

She looked up to find Cutter staring at her.

"What's wrong? Are you not hungry? You don't have to eat now if you don't want to. I just figured…"

Cutter shook his head, looking for a second as if he were too overcome to speak. He cleared his throat.

"This is amazing, that's all. You're amazing. And I'm starving."

They drove home from the club that night without saying much, both of them tired. But it felt like they were in it together, whatever "it" was. Life, maybe?

As exhausted as he was, Cutter still turned to her in bed, taking her with a sleepy enthusiasm she couldn't help but match. No matter how tired she was, she never tired of him.

***

Cutter didn't know what to expect after Emily moved in. Mostly he'd thought about how good it would be to have her with him every night and know he'd never go long without seeing her.

He figured it would be the same as before, just more fun, more Emily. But he'd under-estimated the effect she'd have on his life, how her laughter and soft curses, her distant humming and close murmuring would fill every corner.

Nor did he expect the incredible meals that started appearing regularly. The day after she moved in he came home from a carpentry job, tired and hungry and wishing he didn't have to work at the club that night, and was greeted by the sight of Emily in shorts and a tank top, her hair in a messy knot on her head as she peered down at a cookbook while simultaneously cutting vegetables.

She looked up at him and grinned sheepishly.

"Hey, I hope you don't mind me taking over your kitchen. I'm just so excited to have a real kitchen. I figured we could have a nice meal before work."

"Mind? This is incredible. But you know you don't have to cook for me, right? There are no strings attached to this deal."

"But I want to cook for you. And I'll be enjoying it to, don't you worry."

He came up behind her and put his hands at her waist as he nuzzled her neck. "What can I do to help?"

"I've got it all under control. Just relax. You must be exhausted."

At first he felt bad, like he was taking advantage, but she really did seem to enjoy it. Freed from her hotel room with a big kitchen and someone to cook for, she poured over his cookbooks and browsed cooking websites. She quizzed him on his favorite foods and seemed to take pleasure in surprising him as well.

Meals had never been a particular pleasure when he was growing up. There hadn't been any food to spare at his mom's, and he'd been raised to think of food as fuel to get through the day, nothing more. And his dad was no gourmet. They'd eaten like bachelors, though at least he'd never gone hungry there. Even he and Amy used to eat out all the time, or else heat up soup and eat it while sitting in front of the TV.

Living with Emily made him realize what he'd been missing. Not just in the way of food, but in affection and fun. From the first day she lived there his house became a home, a fact that thrilled and terrified him in equal measure.

Chapter Eight

"Have you thought about looking into one of the ballet companies here? Maybe you really could get a job with one of them."

Emily had just returned from practicing at the club and was still in her leotard and filmy skirt, her damp hair pulled back in a ponytail. She was standing at the counter drinking water, but now she coughed and sputtered.

"I don't think so."

"Why not? Why not look into it and see if they have anything that suits you?" he asked.

"Because I already know they wouldn't." She sighed, hating that he was making her say things that would only made them both feel bad. "I know it may not make sense to you, but I worked my whole life to be in the top companies. The ones here are second rate at best. I just...I'd feel so defeated if I ended up with a company like that, and in a city that doesn't especially value it."

Cutter's expression had closed down, shuttering his reaction.

"Right, I get it. I just thought...never mind."

Turning around he opened the refrigerator door, but she could tell he wasn't really looking at anything. His back was tense, his shoulders rigid.

It was the Thursday of their second week together. She'd been in Las Vegas four weeks and was figuring on staying another two or three more. That was already way longer than she'd initially planned. Hopefully Cutter wouldn't bring this up again. Maybe it was a little weird for both of them that she would be leaving before too long, but it was worse to try to change it.

They were both stiff with each other until he went to work and she was asleep when he came home, but by Friday morning it was like nothing had happened.

"Want to go swimming?" he asked.

She had just opened her eyes and there was Cutter standing by the bed, already up and dressed, bright-eyed and ready for the day.

"If I say yes, will I have to get up this second?"

He laughed. "No, you can take your time. It'll be hot whenever we get there, but the water will feel great."

The thought of diving into cool, clear water had her out of bed within minutes. Digging through her bags she finally came up with a bikini, which she put on under a pair of shorts and a tank top. When she entered the kitchen a few minutes later it was to the sight of Cutter making sandwiches, a small cooler at his feet.

"Wow, you didn't say anything about a picnic," she said, peering over his shoulder. "This is serious."

"Hell, yeah, baby, this is the real deal."

"Can I do anything?"

"Nope, I've got it under control. Plus you already made the brownies I'm throwing in here."

"Mm. I can't wait." Standing on her tiptoes she kissed him on the cheek. "You rock."

"That's right. Don't forget it," he said. He was smiling, but there was an unexpected seriousness to how he looked at her that caught her off guard, and again she was reminded that he wanted her to stay.

She ate a quick bowl of oatmeal, poured her coffee into a travel mug and together they headed to the truck. Lake Mead was about an hour's drive east of Las Vegas, the terrain they drove through scorched looking, but the days were actually a lot cooler now than they had been when she arrived, the hottest part of the day rising only into the mid-eighties.

The mountains surrounding the lake were as stark as the rest of the landscape, but beautiful in their own way, and the lake itself looked cool and inviting. They parked and made their way to Cutter's favorite cove, a little lagoon that was deserted when they got there.

They swam and splashed around for an hour or so before getting out. Emily spread the old blanket Cutter had brought while admiring him as he unpacked the cooler. Even though she had her hands on him every day and night, she still wasn't used to how straight-up beautiful he was.

They sat for a little while after they ate, admiring the view.

"Want to go for a quick hike while we're still wet?"

"Sure. Lead the way."

"Hang on a second," he said, grabbing the tube of sun block from the blanket. "You're starting to burn."

Squeezing lotion onto his fingers, he rubbed it into her back before coming round in front of her to smooth it gently over her face. He gave her a quick smile and kissed her on the nose.

There was something so tender about it, so friendly and caring, that it threw her off guard for a minute. This went beyond sexual attraction to something more profound. She was a lot more comfortable with the lascivious grin he'd given her when she stripped down to her bikini.

"Ready?" he asked, holding a hand out to her, and together they headed back to the car where they stored the cooler before heading up a nearby trail.

At first glance the surroundings seemed barren, but then Cutter began pointing out lizards darting over rocks and different varieties of vegetation, and she saw there was more going on than she realized. Even so, she was mostly on the lookout for rattlesnakes. They'd passed a sign warning of them, and she couldn't help thinking that one was about to dart out and strike at any moment.

"Have you ever seen a rattlesnake?" she asked oh-so-casually as they wound their way along.

"Yeah, once. And I'll admit I was pretty unnerved, but nothing happened. In fact it was kind of amazing. I was walking along through some sagebrush when I heard the rattle. I stopped and looked around, and there was the snake, a couple of feet in front of me. I veered way around it and kept going and that was that."

"Seriously? You didn't pee your pants and decide never to walk in sagebrush again? That's what I'd do."

Cutter laughed. "Actually, I found it reassuring. If it had wanted to attack, it wouldn't have warned me. But they want us to stay away from them. If you're careful and you pay attention, you'll be fine."

So she was paying attention. *Really, really* paying attention, scanning the ground so methodically Cutter had to keep stopping and waiting for her. Of course, he probably thought she was just admiring the native plant and animal life, not being a total neurotic.

They were circling back toward the car when she heard something, something that sounded like a rattle, and then saw movement out of the corner of her eye. Too scared to even make a sound, she ran backward, stumbling over her own feet, in the process stepping down into an empty streambed. She came down hard on her bad foot and let out a yelp of pain as she collapsed on the ground.

Cutter was beside her in a matter of seconds.

"Are you all right? What happened?" he asked, dropping down beside her.

"I heard a rattlesnake," she said, gripping her ankle as she listened fiercely.

"Seriously?"

"Listen. There it is again!"

They both fell silent. Then the noise sounded again.

"Did you hear that?" she asked.

"Actually, that's just the sound of all this dry brush rubbing together when the wind blows."

Emily's mouth dropped open and she felt her face heat by a few more degrees. "You mean I just freaked out over plants blowing around?"

"Afraid so. How bad is your foot?"

"I don't know. It's done this a couple of other times since I injured it. Sometimes I can walk on it right away, and sometimes I can't."

Cutter stood and then helped her up, but pain shot through her foot as soon as she tried to put weight on it. A few choice swears erupted from her and she sagged in defeat.

"You go ahead. Save yourself," she said, trying for humor even though she was furious with herself.

But Cutter was frowning and looking ahead, obviously contemplating the reality of getting back to the car.

"I'm really sorry," she said. "I'm supposed to be graceful and then I go falling over myself –"

"Here, take this," he said, handing her the water bottle he'd been carrying for the two of them.

Before she knew what he was getting at, he bent down and picked her up, one arm under her knees and the other at her back.

"What are you doing? You can't carry me all the way!"

"Sure I can," he said mildly, already walking. "It's probably only a mile or so to the car. Besides, how else do you think we'll get you back? We can't get a car up here."

This was true. She fell silent, swamped with guilt.

Cutter marched along, breathing only a little heavier than usual, though he was soon sweating from the heat.

"I'm sorry I've been eating so much lately," she said meekly. "This would have been easier for you a few weeks ago."

Cutter laughed and kissed her. "You're light as a feather, babe."

He stopped only once to rest, setting her gently on a boulder while he took a breather.

"You could sling me over your shoulder, if that would be easier," Emily offered. "My weight would be distributed –"

Cutter stopped her with a kiss. "Shut up, sweetie," he said kindly.

Picking her up again he continued on. After what felt like forever but was really forty minutes by her watch, they reached the car.

They rode home listening to Emmilou Harris, the inhospitable landscape taking on a whole new meaning for her. She'd never really been in danger, but if she'd hurt herself with anyone else, it would have been a lot messier. He'd carried her out like it was nothing.

She wasn't sure how she felt about being rescued like that. It would almost have been easier if he'd made a big deal out of it, complained or made her feel bad for being so ridiculous. Instead he was...heroic. And it wasn't the first time he'd taken care of her, or even the most dramatic. She'd never met a man she'd have trusted with her life, but here he was beside her, whistling as if it were just another day.

"Thank you," she said, squeezing his hand.

Cutter looked at her, clearly surprised by her intensity.

"It was nothing," he said, trying again to brush it off.

"No, it was definitely something," she replied, and let it go at that.

Emily spent the rest of the afternoon with her foot up, icing it every twenty minutes. When she tried again to stand it was better, and she was able to limp around without much trouble. Hopefully she'd be okay by Sunday night if she took it easy.

Since neither one of them was up for cooking they had pizza delivered. They were just finishing up when Cutter's phone rang.

"It's my mom," he said, sounding glum.

Dutifully he answered, getting up from the table and heading out the back door to talk.

Emily cleared and washed the dishes in the sink, then made her slow way into the kitchen. Glancing out the back door she saw that Cutter was off the phone, but he was still standing out there, his back to the door.

"Everything okay?" she asked, popping her head outside.

He turned around and attempted a smile. "Same as always," he shrugged.

Emily stepped onto the deck and wrapped her arms around his waist. After a few moments she felt him relax into her and a sigh escaped him. Together they stood there as the light slowly faded, neither of them saying a word. She was so immersed in Cutter she wasn't really paying attention to what was out there. When she finally looked out into his back yard, her mouth fell open.

Of course she'd glanced out the back door before, but normally he had the curtains drawn so the sun didn't beat into the house. Plus until the last week or so it had been too damned hot to go outside. Now with dusk falling, softening everything with shadows, it was as if she were seeing his garden for the first time.

Stone paths curved around low bushes and trees, tall decorative grasses, and an incredible variety of cactus plants. Until that moment she'd viewed the native vegetation as dreary, but this was anything but. Unlike the gardens she'd seen around the hotels – lush, vivid arrangements of plants that clearly never grew on their own in Nevada – this was a little paradise out of the desert's own plant life.

"Did you do all that?" she asked him.

"Yeah. I picked a lot up at the nursery I worked for in high school. Anyway, I had to put something back there. It was pretty much just dirt when I moved in. You should see it in March when everything's in bloom."

He stopped then, as if suddenly realizing what he'd said. Because of course she wasn't going to be here in March.

"Why don't you show me around?"

"What about your foot?" he asked. "Shouldn't you take it easy?"

"I'll be fine. If I need to, I'll lean on you," she said. "Come on, you can show off and tell me what all the plants are."

"Okay, if you're sure."

His hand came to rest on her bare arm, supporting her down the stairs, and the simple contact sent a rush of desire through her veins. At the bottom of the steps he took her hand, the way he sometimes did without seeming to think about it.

Together they walked along the stone paths and he named the plants for her – yellow daisies, butterfly and indigo bush, juniper, barrel cacti, agaves, all sorts of tall grasses. He even had a small herb garden. Somehow that awed her as much as anything. She'd never known any man who had such a thing.

All if it brought home more than anything could how rooted he was to this place. Whereas she was rooted to nothing and nowhere.

But it was impossible to feel down in the middle of such unusual beauty. And then there was Cutter himself, the man who'd created it all with such care and devotion. So handsome he was beautiful, so strong he made everything seem easy.

She put her hand on his arm, calling his attention from a plant he was examining.

"You're pretty amazing, you know that?" she said.

He looked surprised. "Anyone could do this if they put the time in."

But Emily was too far gone for talking. Out there with him as the sun went down, she felt herself inexorably drawn toward him.

Birds she didn't recognize sang from the bushes and tall grasses, and she felt all at once like Eve come upon Adam unexpectedly. An Eve who hadn't known there was such a creature in the world.

Reaching up she took his face between her hands, pressing her lips to his. Just that, and yet it shook her to the core, the simplicity of it belying a connection that didn't break when their lips parted, but made separation unbearable.

"Emily," he breathed, and she could see he felt it too.

His lips touched hers again, testing, grazing over her mouth before a soft moan escaped her and the kiss grew deeper, hungrier. Something elemental passed between them, and a need rose in her to connect with him in every way possible. She wanted to breathe in his skin, taste him, feel him along every inch of her, inside her. Together they fell to their knees on the soft blue petals that crept along the ground. She could feel him tremble, feel emotions coursing through him.

His arm came around her and he eased her back until he was on top of her, kissing her eyes, her cheekbones, her throat. Gentle and fierce, he gave her what she needed, pressing her to the earth when she felt as if she might drift up into the darkening sky.

Her hands moved over him, pulling at his clothes until he laughed, a dark, shaky sound of bemusement and desire. Standing up he pulled his shirt over his head, then unbuttoned his shorts and pulled them off with his underwear until he was gloriously naked.

Dropping down beside her, he kissed her deep, a lush, devouring kiss full of promises. Greedily she ran her hands over his smooth skin as she licked the salt from his throat.

His breathing was fast and ragged as he moved down her body, his mouth skimming beneath the neckline of her tank top to lick between her breasts. She opened her legs and lifted her hips in anticipation. He was so good, oh so good with that mouth of his.

Pushing her skirt up her thighs he kissed his way to her center. Then his mouth was on her though her underwear, licking first slow and then faster, light and then with more pressure, until she knew she'd come any second if she didn't stop him.

But she wasn't ready to let go yet, didn't want it to end. She wanted to feel him moving inside her while every nerve ending still screamed for release.

Sitting up, she pushed at his chest until he rolled onto his back.

Standing up, she felt as if the last shreds of civilization left her as her clothes fell to the cooling leaves at her feet. Putting a foot on either side of him she dropped down, lowering herself onto him little by little, driving them both crazy. They moaned in unison as she sank fully onto him and he slid into her wet heat. She leaned over him and kissed him deep, whimpers of pleasure rising from her as he drove into her with no barrier between them.

Sitting up he took a breast in his mouth, his eyes closed, lashes dark against his dusky skin. She spread her knees to take him deeper, each thrust hitting home with an ache so sweet it was almost painful.

She was almost there, had been the moment she took him inside her. Now she was strung too tight, her body crying out for release. As if knowing how close she was, Cutter slid a thumb onto her clit, the direct pressure so intense her head fell back and one hand gripped his thigh. All at once her release swept through her with the heat and power of stars being born.

She was still gasping when he flipped her beneath him with a neat roll, never leaving her. Then he pushed her thighs against her chest and drove into her, sleek and hard, so big she felt another wave rise up and take her away just as he groaned and kissed her again.

She must have dozed off. She awoke under an indigo sky, limitless and unfathomable. Cutter woke the next instant and together they stumbled to their feet. But she held back, lingering for one last minute in the dark of his garden, wishing they could stay there under the stars, away from hard questions and confusion. Then she put her hand in his and followed him to the house and into his bed.

***

Cutter came awake the next morning suffused with a feeling of well-being. He lay there for long minutes remembering last night, but soon he wanted the real thing.

He opened his eyes only to realize that Emily was already up. Sunlight flooded the room and washed over his bed because he'd been too out of it to close the blinds last night. No doubt that was what had woken her.

The faint hum of music and smell of coffee pulled him out of bed. He pulled on last night's shorts and headed down the hall.

She was leaning against the sofa, her back to him, dressed only in a black camisole and bikini underwear, her hair loose and mussed. At first he was so struck by the picture she made he didn't hear what she was saying.

"I was surprised too, but they said they can spare me now," Emily was saying. "If I leave Tuesday I should be in Boston sometime Friday."

Cutter forgot to breathe. Had he heard her right? Was she really leaving in three days?

He was still standing there when Emily said goodbye and turned around. Her mouth fell open and she looked at him with a mixture of dismay and guilt that knocked the breath out of him.

"I guess you heard all that."

"Are you seriously leaving Tuesday?"

"I'm sorry. I know it's sudden –"

"Hell yeah, it's sudden. What happened to staying another few weeks?"

Emily bit her lip, her big blue eyes looking at him with such resigned sadness he felt his stomach drop to his knees.

"Things are getting more serious than either one of us expected. The longer I stay, the harder it's going to be for both of us when I leave."

"Then don't leave."

"Please don't make this harder than it is," she said, her voice pleading. "I can't give you want you want. What you deserve. I don't want to hurt you, but if I get distracted and stay here, I may never get my life back. I've already stayed here too long. There's an apartment waiting for me, people waiting for me. I can't drop all that just because I've been happy here with you."

"But why not stay if you're happy? Isn't that what you want?" he asked, the knowledge that he was losing her seeping like ice water into his veins.

"I can't afford to chose it over the rest of my life. It's already made me complacent. I should have left here weeks ago but I didn't want...I didn't want to leave you. But I'll never forgive myself if I stay, and I'll resent you too."

Cutter looked at her, his body tense with frustration and the effort it took to hold back all he wanted to say. His jaw ached from clenching it too tightly, holding in the howl of pain he wanted to let loose. A thousand replies went through his head, but she'd rendered all of them pointless.

They stood there facing each other, neither of them saying anything for a moment. Then Emily roughly wiped her eyes.

"I don't even know why you want me," she said, confusion and weariness in her voice. "I'm a disaster. For all you know all I'll ever be is a stripper."

"Jesus, Emily. I didn't fall in love with what you do for a living."

He hadn't even admitted it to himself until just this moment, but now that he'd said it he was relieved. He was all in now. If Emily didn't want him, it wouldn't be because he hadn't tried.

She was staring at him, clearly shocked.

"I don't know what to say."

Which pretty much said it all. He could feel a trainload of pain bearing down on him, but he wasn't going under with her around to witness it.

"You don't need to say anything. It's not your fault. But I think it would be better if you went back to the hotel for your last few days."

He felt dizzy, shocked by his own request but unwilling to back down. He couldn't be in the same house with her anymore. It would kill him.

Emily started to say something and then stopped. Her eyes were wide with the same disbelief he felt. As he watched they filled with tears.

"If that's what you want," she said, biting her lip.

"It's the last thing I want."

"I'm sorry. I never thought..." she began. But now she was crying in earnest and fool that he was, he wanted to comfort her.

"I'm sorry, too." He grabbed his wallet and keys from the counter, determined to leave before he made a fool out of himself. But he couldn't help looking at her one more time, his teary-eyed dancer standing in his kitchen, looking as bereft as he felt.

God, he loved her.

He walked out, shutting the door quietly behind him.

Chapter Nine

Emily drove back to the hotel feeling like she might die. She cried so hard she couldn't catch her breath, and she got lost three times even though she'd been driving the same route nearly every day for the last two weeks.

She held it together while she checked back into the hotel, and then she fell into bed and cried. Somehow she'd really thought it would be easier to leave sooner rather than later, but they were far past the point of avoiding pain.

She'd never imagined he could love her. Turning away from that was the hardest thing she'd ever done. Part of her wanted it, rejoiced in it, and the other part knew it was far too dangerous. Her feelings for him were already overwhelming, even when kept in check. If set loose, they'd keep her here forever.

But all the rationalizing in the world couldn't fill the aching hollow in her chest or ease the sickening feeling in the pit of her stomach. She woke the next morning, headachey and exhausted, and nearly called in and quit so that she didn't have to dance that night. But she couldn't do it. As awful as it would feel to see Cutter now, it was worlds better than never seeing him again.

She got to the club early and told Steve she was leaving. The manager was none too pleased, especially seeing as she was only giving him a days' notice, but he'd get over it. There were always more girls.

"Are you all right?" Cheryl asked as they sat side by side in front of the mirror getting ready.

Emily was trying to cover her bruised-looking eyes with mediocre results.

"Not really, but I'll survive," she replied, giving what she hoped looked like a smile before turning back to the mirror.

Thank God Cheryl seemed to take the hint and said no more, though a couple of the other girls asked her the same thing. They seemed genuinely sorry to hear she was leaving, but also curious. They all knew about her and Cutter – how could they not? – and they rightly figured things had gone sour.

Maybe Cheryl would get her shot with Cutter after all.

By the time Emily went on for her first set she was a wreck, nauseated and shaking, worse than any stage fright she'd ever endured. All she could think about was Cutter out there, so close by and yet by her own design unreachable. Her sore foot only added to her misery, the physical pain undermining her usual confidence in her abilities.

She hadn't thought through what it would be like to strip with him there, and the reality of it was worse than anything she could have prepared for. For the first time Cutter didn't look at her at all, and she didn't want him to. She'd always danced for him, and with that gone the veil between the fantasy she'd always been able to spin for herself and the customers fell away. It took everything she had to keep going, everything she had not to run off the stage.

There was no way she could face Cutter while working the floor, nor could she have composed herself enough to flirt with the customers, so instead she hid in the dressing room between sets.

She ran into him anyway in the hallway backstage after her last dance. She was exhausted and demoralized, worn down from performing rather than exhilarated by it, and dressed in just a gold thong and stilettos, her hair wild and sweaty. She'd always felt sexy when she was in costume around Cutter, but now her exaggerated sexuality seemed to mock them both.

She could hardly look at him.

"You doing all right?" he asked.

"I've been better," she said, her throat closing as tears threatened.

"Yeah, me, too. But I suppose we'll live, right?" he said bitterly. His shuttered eyes took her in while giving nothing back.

"I suppose so," she replied, at a loss how to respond to this new side of him.

But she needn't have worried because he didn't stick around long enough for more conversation. Without another word he turned and walked away.

She very nearly left town right then. The urge to get in her car and start driving was so intense, she had to close her eyes and breathe for several minutes before reason returned.

She'd wait until morning and then see how she felt. She was in no shape to do anything more tonight. She went back to her hotel and showered, tired beyond telling but too wired to still her mind. She slept only a few hours in the end, waking up shortly after sunrise. For a few blessed moments she remembered nothing, and then it all came flooding back to her.

But she'd stay another day. She and Cutter hadn't said a real goodbye, and they both deserved better than what they'd managed last night.

Getting up, she tore around her room, re-packing the bags she'd packed so haphazardly when leaving Cutter's house. Afterward she rode the elevator down to one of the restaurants and sat reading the paper as she ate breakfast, drawing the event out so as to fill as much time as possible.

By mid-morning she'd just about lost it and decided to take refuge in her lifelong routine. In a matter of minutes she was in her practice clothes and entering the club. She said hello to the cleaning crew, grateful that no one else she knew was there, and flipped on the lights illuminating the stage.

Pulling a chair to the side she began her barre warm-up, carefully emptying her mind of everything but what she was calling on her body to do. She counted, focused on her line, bent into her pliés , grateful as always that her body could still do this much. After a time she moved the chair out of the way and did her center floor warm-up, executing careful pirouettes and tendues, gradually increasing the tempo. All of it on demi pointe, since wearing pointe shoes was a thing of the past.

When she was good and limber she walked over to the audio system to plug in her iPod, but instead of choosing the Wynton Marsalis song she was choreographing to, she scrolled through until she got to a classical piece she'd once danced to, a modern work that had been choreographed on her just after she arrived in San Francisco.

Wondering if she was making a mistake but unable to stop herself, she pressed play and walked out onto the stage. Then the first strains of the music sounded – the low mournful sound of strings and woodwinds – and her body started moving, the steps so much a part of her that even now, three years later, she didn't have to reach for them.

All the longing of the piece mixed with her own feelings until she didn't know where she ended and the choreographer's intention began. And there was something else, a new understanding flowing through her, a deeper meaning she hadn't found when she'd danced it before.

All her confusion and pain found their way into each step until the dance felt richer and more authentic than anything she'd done before. She gave herself over to the steps and the music, let her heart open and let it break, feeling for the first time what she'd only glimpsed every other time before.

She'd danced it well back then. It had been considered one of her finest roles, and yet she'd never understood it fully until now.

The last note sounded, a piercingly bittersweet note that hung in the air. Emily held her arabesque until the sound dissipated into the stale air of the club, her chest heaving. She felt depleted and wrung out, yet as clear-headed as she'd ever been.

She loved him.

The thought itself, once it settled on her, was no surprise at all. It had been there all along, waiting for her to recognize it. This new feeling in her dancing, this new depth – loving him had made her a better artist. She hadn't known it was possible, could never have guessed it. Even the dance she was choreographing had begun to change in the past weeks, with new undercurrents that made it richer and more nuanced.

She stood in the middle of the stage, her mind racing. All along she'd thought she had to choose between Cutter and her dreams, happiness and her art. But they were one, entwined together in the best possible way.

She couldn't leave him. How had she ever thought that was possible? Happiness was staring her in the face and she'd turned away from it, her vision so narrow she hadn't seen what she was letting go. Maybe she'd lose money on the apartment she'd rented, but she could live with that. She couldn't live without Cutter, so it was no contest.

The only thing she really felt bad about was her mother. Her mom would definitely be disappointed Emily wasn't coming home, but she'd understand. She always did.

Grabbing her phone she started to call Cutter, but something made her stop. If she was going to live here, she needed some kind of plan. They both needed to know how their lives would work together, and Cutter deserved something well-thought out and considered, something believable.

Heading to the hotel business center she sat at a computer and looked up the job postings for the Las Vegas Ballet Company and Nevada Ballet Theater. Neither had jobs open for anything near what she'd be qualified for. But then she looked at NBT's upcoming performances and saw that she'd performed half the dances they were doing in the upcoming season. Surely they could use someone like her to help stage the ballets or teach?

She didn't have a résumé, so she spent the next two hours creating one from scratch. When she had something halfway decent she ran up to her room to change and then downstairs where she paced the lobby, waiting for the valet to bring her car around. Her head was spinning at the idea that she and Cutter loved one another, that she was so close to having him.

If he hadn't given up on her that is. If he wasn't so angry or hurt that he didn't want her anymore.

Her very life seemed to hang in the balance and her body hummed with fear and exhilaration. It was nearly after three when she arrived at the building that housed Nevada Ballet Theater. Now she just had to hope someone would talk to her.

Luck was on her side. The receptionist frowned at her for walking in off the street, but when she looked at her resume her expression changed.

"Wait just a moment," she said, picking up the phone. "The artistic director just got out of a meeting. I'll try to catch her."

Emily's heart pounded as she looked around. They were essentially in the middle of the main hallway, and dancers passed by, talking and laughing. For a second she wondered if she could handle being back in a company and not dancing. It was the reason she'd avoided the idea for so long.

It was tradition for retired dancers to teach when their careers were over. The art form depended on dancers passing down what they knew. But on the rare occasions she'd let herself think about it at all, she'd imagined herself far older, teaching at the San Francisco Ballet or one of the other top companies in the country.

But she had to look beyond the idea of prestige. No, this wasn't a world-class company, but then she had no experience teaching or choreographing. She'd be lucky to get a job at a place like this. Besides, the people here would love dance just as much as they did in New York or Paris.

The receptionist put the phone down.

"Ms. Wallace can spare a few moments to meet you. Take the elevator to the forth floor and you'll see her office."

Emily stepped out of the elevator clutching her purse and résumé. Another receptionist sat inside the artistic director's office, and she nodded and waved her on.

"Ms. Chase?"

The director looked up from her desk and smiled, gesturing to a chair opposite her. Emily sat, nervously clasping her hands in her lap.

"I understand you're interested in a job here?"

"Yes, that's right," she said, standing up and handing over her résumé before sitting again. "I've danced many of the ballets you're performing this season. I'm hoping there's a role for me here, perhaps staging or teaching."

Emily held her breath as Ms. Wallace looked at her résumé and then back up at her.

"What brings you to Las Vegas?"

"I had to retire due to an injury and I've been staying with a friend here. I've just decided to stay permanently."

"I was very sorry to hear about your injury. You're a beautiful dancer. I'm sure it's been a hard time for you."

Emily stared for a moment, shocked that this woman had known about her.

"Thank you. It's been an adjustment, but I'm managing. And I very much want to be part of a company again in some way."

"I take it you don't have any teaching experience?"

"I've taught roles to other dancers, and I feel my professional experience will be more than enough to teach," Emily replied, trying to sound calm and confident.

"More than likely," Ms. Wallace said. "I have an instructor going on maternity leave in two months, so I could certainly use someone to fill in for her. As for staging, I'd love to take you on in a part-time capacity if I can come up with the funds. That's something I'd have to look into, and we'd start on a trial basis. But first things first. How do you feel about teaching a couple of small classes while someone observes? That'll give us an idea how you'll do."

"That would be fine," Emily said, amazed.

"Good. Someone will give you a call in the next week or so to arrange it."

Emily stood and thanked her. She managed to keep her cool until she was alone in the elevator. Then she jumped up and down, grinning from ear to ear.

She had to tell Cutter, but it was already four-thirty. She had just enough time to get back to the hotel and get her things together for tonight. If she was lucky, she'd catch him before she had to go on.

Giddy with anxiety, she got into her car and drove. She arrived at the club well before six to change and wait for Cutter, frantically leaving the dressing room over and over to look for him. But he didn't show up until just before she had to go on, leaving her no time to talk to him.

Should she write him a note? No, that was silly. But the last thing she wanted was a repeat of last night. She needed some way to let him know how she felt.

***

Cutter got to the club mid-morning on Monday to finish the shelving units Steve had commissioned for the basement storage area. He'd just finished hauling in all the wood when he heard classical music come on upstairs.

Emily.

His skin heated and his heart started pounding at the thought that she was in the same building. He'd thought it was safe, and now here he was again, thrown into a tailspin.

What was she doing here? There was no reason for her to be practicing on her last day, but something had obviously driven her to come.

He tried to keep working, tried to shut out the image of her up there in her practice clothes, the fine hairs at the nape of her neck damp with sweat. But he was as powerless to stop himself from going up as a moth heading for a flame. He climbed the stairs with a mixture of anticipation and dread, only to come to a dead stop in the shadows at the room's edge, stunned by the sight of Emily dancing her heart out, her face a wrenching combination of joy and sorrow.

The dancing he'd seen her do, which was always head and shoulders better than anyone else, was still nothing compared to this. Her dancing for the club left him throbbing with lust. This made his heart ache.

Watching her, seeing the look on her face, he suddenly understood what he'd been up against. Of course she couldn't be satisfied here, with him. He'd been a fool to think otherwise. The music ended and she stood there, gazing out into the dark room, more beautiful than any woman he'd ever seen. As untouchable as a figment of his imagination.

He turned and walked out, wondering if the pain of losing her would ever go away. Even though part of him was still angry with her for not loving him back, the best part of him hoped she'd find what she needed someday soon.

It was plain masochism to work tonight. But as awful as it promised to be, it was better than the alternative.

He finished the shelves by early afternoon and then headed to the gym. It would do him good to work out, but if he were honest with himself, he was also avoiding his house. Memories of Emily laughing, teasing, driving him crazy with need were in every room.

He didn't get back to the club until the last possible moment, and his whole body was tense knowing that any minute she was going to come on. He couldn't bear watching her dance up there, and he couldn't stand not watching.

Then Stan announced her and all the regulars went wild knowing they were in for a treat. Though he wasn't sure if that would be the case. He'd avoided watching her last night but had gleaned enough to know she'd struggled through her sets. Maybe it would have been better if he'd stayed away tonight, but it seemed he was past being able to choose the right course of action.

Then the first song began and he felt sick. It was Nina Simone's "Turn Me On," a short, crooning tune that he and Emily had once made love to. Memories of that night came flooding back – the way her hair had spilled over his chest in a silky pool, the way they'd moved together so perfectly she'd declared afterward that a choreographer couldn't have improved on it. Just before she'd fallen asleep she'd murmured that he'd ruined her for anyone else. He'd even started to believe her.

Had she forgotten about that night? He could think of no other reason she'd choose that song. She'd never been deliberately cruel.

Confusion and despair surged through him, but he wouldn't look at her. He didn't know what was happening, but he wasn't going to be part of it.

He was heading for the far end of the room, his back to the stage, when a scuffle broke out in the front of the room – a couple of drunk guys at the edge of the stage fighting over the skimpy red top Emily had tossed. Cutter took it from them, settling that quick enough, but now he was holding her sexy little costume. He was still holding it when the first song ended and the Stones' "You Got the Silver" started to play, the same song he and Emily had danced to in his kitchen the day he'd asked her to move in.

Cutter looked up at Emily, only several feet away.

She was looking right at him.

It was so like all the other times she'd danced for him, teasing him throughout the night, only this time her expression was serious as she moved sinuously to the music, echoing the way she'd danced that morning. It was no mistake. She was doing it for a reason. But what was she trying to say?

She'd stripped down to just her thong, her gorgeous body whirling around the stage, though every time she looked out at the crowd it was him she looked at. And though his body ached with desire, it was his heart that ached more. Hope rose in him as their eyes stayed locked, and he waited to see what message her last song would bring.

A surprised laugh escaped him as Frank Zappa's "Tell Me You Love Me" poured out of the speakers. She'd once come upon him installing a new light fixture in the foyer while this song blared through the house.

"Who's this?" she'd yelled, trying to make herself heard.

"Zappa," he called back, turning the volume down so they didn't have to yell. "Sorry, is it too loud?"

"I like it," she said, smiling at him with that look in her eye that always made him hard. "The world needs more kick-ass love songs."

Now he watched as she moved around the stage, dancing to one of his favorite songs, the audience going wild. It was the sexiest performance he'd seen so far, and it was all for him. It might as well have been just the two of them in the room, because he knew now what she was telling him.

The second she left the stage he made for the door to the back hallway, pushing his way past patrons, past a couple of dancers, past Steve. Nothing was going to keep him from her a second longer.

***

Emily watched Cutter come toward her, relief flooding her at his hungry expression. She'd had a whole speech prepared, but looking at him it all flew out of her head. Instead she launched herself at him, throwing her arms around his neck.

"I love you," she told him between kisses. "I love you I love you I love you. I'm sorry I was such an idiot."

Cutter's mouth closed over hers, his tongue sliding into her with all the heat and intimacy she'd come to crave. Holding her to his hard-muscled body, he devoured her with his mouth and hands, a primal groan rising from his throat.

A few people passed by them, hooting and cheering. Someone, it sounded like Richie, suggested they get a room.

"Good idea," Cutter said, coming up for air.

Taking Emily by the hand he pulled her toward the storage closet. Opening it up he ushered her inside and then followed, closing the rest of the world out as he shut the door behind them.

"Does this mean you're staying?" he asked her, his hands gripping her shoulders.

She cupped his face in her hands, needing to touch him.

"Nothing could make me leave now."

"But what about your career and not wanting to compromise?"

"The only compromise would be if I left you. This is where I want to be."

"I saw you dance this morning," he said.

"You were here? Today?"

He nodded his head, his dark eyes looking straight into hers. "I think I get now what dancing means to you, and I don't want you to have to settle. I sure as hell don't want you to keep stripping. If there are more opportunities for you somewhere else, we can move."

"It may take a while to get my feet under me, but that would be the case anywhere. I think I have a good shot here. It's not going to be full-time, at least not for a while, so I'll need to work here for a bit longer. But as long as you're in the audience, I'll be fine. More than fine."

"Then so will I."

Bending his head he kissed her again. A slow, exploratory kiss, as if he were discovering her all over again. She melted into it, into him, wanting everything he had to give.

His arms came around her pulling her to him, the mixture of tenderness and desire leaving her boneless. Her hands threaded through his hair, holding him to her as he showed her how much he wanted her, his tongue stroking again and again over hers. His strength and heat engulfed her, reminding her how good they were together and how close she'd come to blowing it.

She slid her hands down his arms and under his shirt to feel the smooth skin over hard muscle.

"Hey, Cutter?" she said, pulling back a fraction of an inch.

"Yeah?" he began kissing her neck, his hands closing over her breasts.

She was practically naked already, and she could feel Cutter's enormous erection pressing against her belly. Desire was spreading through her, laying waste to all rational thought. But she had enough coherence left for one last effort.

"Lock the door."

About the Author

Isabel began reading romances at the age of fourteen. That's the year her grandmother came to visit, bringing with her a shopping bag filled with (very tame) Harlequin and Silhouette romance novels. Isabel was immediately and forever hooked. What could be better than experiencing all that lust and new love just by reading a book?

Sign up for Isabel's Newsletter[1] at www.isabelmorin.com[2] and get new release alerts and exclusive content. Your email address will never be shared, and you can unsubscribe at any time.

Email Isabel at isabel@isabelmorin.com. She'd love to hear from you!

---

1. http://eepurl.com/ddvys5

2. http://www.isabelmorin.com